Hero

Rescue Team

Heronsway
Rescue Team

Elizabeth Wynne

An Armada Original

First published in Armada in 1989

Armada is an imprint of the Children's Division,
part of the Collins Publishing Group,
8 Grafton Street, London W1X 3LA

Printed and bound in Great Britain by
William Collins Sons & Co. Ltd, Glasgow

Conditions of Sale

"I've never seen him out *this* far before!"

"Where does he live?" Sandy asked Tessa, her eyes on the distant figure. The old man was bending down at the roadside, holding a large black plastic bag.

"In the village," Tessa replied. "He's got a tiny cottage, up a sort of alley-way, next to the supermarket. You might not have seen it," she added, "Hunter's Lane, it's called – it's a very old bit of Clereton."

As they neared him on their ponies, the two girls could see that the old man was tearing with one hand at the long grass on the verge, and pushing it into the bag which he held with the other. "I wonder what he wants the grass for," Sandy said.

Tessa Roberts leaned over from Duskie's saddle and spoke conspiratorially, as they neared the stooping figure. "His animals," she told her friend. "He's a grumpy old thing," she confided. "He seems to like animals better than people – takes on all the unwanted pets."

"Well, I think that's —" But Sandy was cut off in mid-sentence by Quest, who now demanded all her attention. The pony had come to a halt, her beautiful chestnut head thrown high, her nostrils distended. She quivered, her whole body poised for flight.

"Uh-uh!" Tessa reined in Duskie, her black pony, who was placid in comparison to his spirited chestnut companion. "The moorland menace is up to her tricks again! I think she's about to take off, Sandy," she added, looking askance at her friend. "See you back at the equestrian centre!"

"It's all right, girlie," Sandy crooned, smoothing the trembling chestnut neck, soothingly. "It's only a silly old plastic bag. You *know* they always rustle like that."

Quest snorted, loud and long, pushing her nose into the air. She took one cautious step forward, watching the bag closely. The old man continued with his grass-pulling.

"He's a bit deaf," Tessa hissed. She cleared her throat. "Good evening, Mr Crichley!" she shouted.

The old man turned his head stiffly to look at them, and then returned to his task. The grunt that he gave could have been an acknowledgement or maybe just annoyance at being disturbed.

Meanwhile, Quest crept past the dreaded black bag, crab-wise. Keeping her eyes firmly fixed on the crackling plastic, she moved her hindquarters sideways down the road. At last, satisfied that the danger had been passed, Quest began a high-stepping sideways jog down the lane, away from the old man.

Tessa and Duskie followed on, with a more normal gait.

"That pony of yours is such a flighty creature," Tessa remarked, as she and Duskie caught up with their companions. She patted Duskie's shining black neck. "You have your moments, don't you, Duskie, but Quest . . ."

6

Sandy just smiled to herself. Tessa's words were a delight to her ears. "That pony of *yours*," she had said. Eleven-year-old Sandy Corfield's heart sang. Quest *was* hers – for the next year, anyway. Admittedly, the beautiful fourteen-two chestnut mare actually belonged to Kay Carter, who lived and worked in the city. But Kay was pregnant and had been advised by her doctor not to ride, so for the next year Quest was on temporary loan to Sandy.

The two ponies jogged on quietly down the lane which cut straight across the moors. The moorland road was a narrow grey ridge with a deep ditch on one side and a river on the other. Between the road and water, on either side, was a grass verge. Beside the water stood pollarded willows, leaning over the river as if to view their own reflections in the murky water. Beyond were the luxuriant summer fields, grazed by sheep. The grass verges were bright with wild flowers and the field hedges were thick and dense.

"It's perfect, isn't it?" Sandy sighed, breaking the silence.

"What is?"

"Here; the moors, the equestrian centre, holidays – everything!"

"Great!" agreed the more prosaic Tessa, "especially the holidays. No more school for six weeks!"

To celebrate, the girls urged their ponies to canter along a wider part of the grass verge, reining in when they came to the little grey stone bridge which linked the lane with a field beyond the river. Here, occasionally, they saw a heron, standing motionless in the rushes – a thin, hunchbacked figure, solitary and vigilant.

The girls walked their ponies back to the equestrian centre on a loose rein, letting them cool down for the last half mile. Quest, her plastic bag fright forgotten, walked with an easy, swinging stride, while her rider discussed with Tessa the forthcoming gymkhana which was being organized by Sue Venables. Sue, together with her husband, Peter, owned and ran Heronsway Equestrian Centre, where both ponies were stabled.

"Sue seems very busy with it," Sandy commented.

"She says she wants to liven up Clereton a bit," Tessa told her. Leaning forward to flick off a particularly persistent fly which was bothering Duskie, she added, "It's going to be quite a large affair, I think."

"I'm looking forward to it," Sandy admitted.

"Especially the jumping!"

"Yes, I think we're going to enjoy the jumping, aren't we, Quest?" Sandy smiled as she leaned over to smooth the chestnut's neck. Quest flicked back an ear in response. Recently, with the help of Quest's fast and bold jumping, Sandy had been an important member of the Heronsway Equestrian Centre's team. Heronsway had won a coveted cup for a three-day event, organized by another equestrian centre.

The ponies turned in at the entrance to Heronsway. They walked down the cinder track towards the two-sided stable block, in front of which stood the practice area. Sue Venables was giving a dressage lesson to one of her older pupils. Concentrating on her lesson, Sue gave a cursory wave in the girls' direction.

"Look, there's Adam," Tessa said, pointing towards the stable block. "Let's see if his pony's come yet."

The two girls walked their ponies over towards Adam. But when they arrived beside him, it was obvious from the restlessness in Adam Maiyer's brown eyes, which searched the lane endlessly, that the long-awaited pony had not yet arrived.

"What time's she coming?" Tessa asked, jumping down from Duskie's saddle.

Whenever twelve-year-old Adam was agitated or excited in any way he had a habit of pushing back his thick fringe of dark brown hair. Now, with a quick movement, he pushed it back twice. The girls could see the mixture of excitement and impatience in his normally serious eyes.

"I don't know," he admitted. "That Fiona girl —" his voice was scornful "— she didn't know exactly when she could get the horsebox." His face relaxed into a smile. "But it's going to be today – her father promised."

"Did your dad look at the pony?" Tessa asked.

"Oh yes!" Adam grinned. "I can't imagine Dad not thoroughly inspecting any animal that *we* take on!" Adam's father was a vet – a widower with a busy country practice.

During the recent three-day event, Adam had watched with anger the poor treatment of a bay pony, owned by a member of another team which had taken part. He had been overjoyed when his father had said that he would buy the pony for him.

"We're going on a long ride tomorrow," Tessa told Adam. "Do you want to come?"

Adam looked doubtful. "I think I'll see how

Cinnamon settles in," he explained. "I'll just take her round the lanes tomorrow."

"It'll just be us, then," said Tessa, turning to Sandy, "since Sarah and Andrea are away."

"Our first proper ride of the summer holidays." Sandy heaved a huge sigh of contentment as she slid down from Quest's saddle and patted the chestnut pony enthusiastically. "I'm afraid I shan't be able to wait to see Cinnamon arrive," she added, turning to Adam. "I've promised Mum I'll put in some extra sweet-packaging this evening, since I'll be away all day tomorrow."

Sandy's mother ran a sweet and newspaper shop, single-handed, with some help from her daughter. Sandy's main job was the weighing, packaging and pricing of sweets. In the term-time she did this on Saturday afternoons, in readiness for the following week. Now that the summer holidays had arrived, this pocket-money task had been put forward to Friday. However, this week Sandy would be packing the sweets on Thursday.

"Cinnamon - is that what you're going to call her?" Tessa asked Adam.

Adam frowned slightly. "Well," he said, slowly, "that's what that girl Fiona called her, but I thought I'd call her Cindy."

"That's nice," said Sandy. "It'll sound like her old name. It won't confuse her."

"That's what *I* thought."

"I hope she settles in well," Sandy added, setting off for stable number eight, with Quest ambling beside her. Reaching the stable, Sandy led Quest in through the open doorway. Then, bolting the door behind her, she began unsaddling, whilst the

10

chestnut pony nudged her gently with her soft nose. Sandy stopped for a moment to caress the soft nose and rub Quest behind her ears, as the joy of ownership – however temporary – swept over her again.

"We're going to have all the summer holidays together, Questie," she murmured in the chestnut pony's ear. "It's going to be great!"

2

"What kept you?"

Tessa's head was looking over the half-open lower door of Duskie's stable. Her face was pink with exertion and her fair hair was liberally sprinkled with straw.

"Tess! We *are* on holiday!" As Sandy paused for a moment outside Duskie's stable, a shrill whinny sounded from the other block of stabling. The sound of hoof scraping stable floor echoed around the stable area, as Quest pawed the ground impatiently.

"I think it wants attention!" Tessa commented, drily, before bending down again to attack the dirty straw with renewed vigour.

"Weather's OK for our ride, anyway," Sandy called, as she set off in answer to the summons from Quest.

Tessa paused and poked her head over the door again. She squinted at the sky. "Mm," she said, a little doubtfully, "a bit *too* bright, if you ask me."

"She's just a pessimist, isn't she, girlie?" Sandy said to the chestnut mare, letting herself into Quest's stable and putting her arm around the pony's neck affectionately. "We're going to have a great ride today!"

Sandy led Quest out of the stable and put her with Duskie in the practice area. The chestnut mare trotted round the small enclosure, shaking her head, glad to be able to stretch her limbs. Meanwhile, Sandy set to work in the stable.

"I don't see Cinnamon anywhere," Sandy commented, when the two girls met up at the muck heap.

"She didn't come," Tessa stated, tipping out her barrow-load.

Sandy leaned against her spade. "What happened?" she asked incredulously.

Tessa shrugged her shoulders. "She's not very reliable, that Fiona girl," she said, grasping the handles of her wheelbarrow. "The horsebox wouldn't start, or something. She promised to send her today."

"Poor Adam," Sandy commented, tipping her contribution of droppings and soiled straw out onto the heap.

Soon the two ponies were groomed and saddled.

"Right!" said Tessa, jumping into Duskie's saddle. "Burlington Down, here we come!"

The moors were bright and sparkling fresh in the summer morning light. The ponies, eager and glad to be out, trotted along the lane. Quest danced sideways when a moorhen moved in the rushes.

"Watch out," warned Tessa. "There's a lot of traffic here at this time in the morning."

"All late for work, I suppose," said Sandy, putting her pony on a tighter rein. She leaned forward and spoke firmly: "Behave yourself, Quest." Turning back to Tessa, she added, "That last car was a bit close – the little red one."

13

"Too fast for these lanes, too," commented Tessa.

"It's usually so quiet," said Sandy.

"It's just the to and from work time," Tessa replied. "It'll be back to tractors and old trundlers soon!"

They continued on down the lane in silence for a while. Then Sandy spoke again. "Look!" she said, pointing ahead. "He must be out here again."

"Who?"

"The old man – old Mr Crichley."

Tessa's gaze followed the line of Sandy's pointing finger. "That's odd," she said slowly.

"What is?"

"Well, old Mr Crichley's bag – but no old Mr Crichley."

"Mm. I see what you mean."

Tessa reined in Duskie and looked down at the black bag. It lay on the edge of the grass verge. Quest eyed it suspiciously, but since it wasn't moving or rustling she decided not to take evasive action.

"Can you hold Duskie a minute?" Tessa asked.

"What's the matter?"

"I don't know," Tessa replied as she jumped down from the saddle. Tessa's eyes looked worried as she handed over the reins to Sandy. "But look," she added, turning to point towards the plastic bag, "there's all the greenstuff that he's collected – it's strewn over the verge."

"Do you think —"

"I daren't think," said Tessa, grimly, "but I'm going to investigate."

Following the line of the dropped leaves and grass, Tessa hurried across the verge and peered down into the deep ditch. Sandy heard her give a gasp and when she turned back her face was pale.

"Sandy, we've got to get help – quickly!"

"Is it him?"

"Yes," Tessa answered, her voice cold with anger, "and he didn't just *fall* in there – I think he's been hit by a car. I don't think we should move him," she added. "He's unconscious, and he may have broken something. But we must get help!"

Quickly, Sandy reacted. Thrusting Duskie's reins towards Tessa, she said, "I'll go. Quest's fast, and we can canter on the verge. I'll telephone from the centre."

As Sandy dug her heels into her pony's sides, she heard Tessa's anxious voice. "Hurry, Sandy, *please!*"

Startled by the urgency and harshness of Sandy's leg aids, Quest leapt away at a sharp canter. "Sorry, girl," Sandy murmured, "but we must get back – quickly. Go as fast as you can, Quest!"

Sandy leaned forward, feeling Quest's long fine mane blowing against her face. She gave the pony its head and Quest seemed to sense the urgency. With her neck stretched and her ears back, she travelled back towards the equestrian centre at a gallop along the grass verge. No more vehicles appeared on the road. The red car driver must have been the last of the late traffic, Sandy decided. With relief, she saw the entrance to the equestrian centre and easing on the reins, she slowed the chestnut mare to a fast trot.

At the office door, Sandy leapt off Quest's back.

Still holding the reins, she pushed open the office door and called to Sue.

"There's been an accident. An old man on the moors – by the old stone bridge. We need an ambulance!"

Sandy walked Quest back along the lane. It was a relief to have passed on the urgency to someone else. Sue was efficient. She would soon arrange things, Sandy thought, and as she thought it Sue passed by in the Land-Rover. Sandy saw a pile of rugs on the seat beside her. Trust Sue! She thought of everything. Those would be to keep the old man warm while help was coming.

Sandy and Quest reached Tessa and Sue at the same time as the police car. One of the policemen jumped out and hurried across to look into the ditch, when Tessa had pointed it out.

"The ambulance won't be long," he told them. His eyes were casting around the scene. "Looks like a case of hit and run," he said. "Any idea who did it?" He looked round at the two girls.

"The last car we saw was a red one," Tessa said.

"Going too fast," Sandy added.

The ambulance arrived and the next ten minutes were taken up with gently transferring the old man from the ditch to the ambulance.

As the men manoeuvred the stretcher up from the ditch, old Mr Crichley began to come round. He slightly turned his face, which was streaked with blood. His eyes flickered and opened, and the girls could see his mouth moving.

Tessa handed over Duskie's reins to Sandy and

16

bent down to the old man. "It's all right, Mr Crichley. You'll be warm and safe soon," she told him.

The old man's lips moved again. "He's trying to say something," Sandy said.

Tessa listened carefully. The old man spoke in a hoarse whisper.

"We'll have to keep moving," said one of the ambulance men. "Must get him to hospital as soon as possible."

"What did he say?" Sandy asked Tessa, as the stretcher was turned and placed gently but quickly inside the ambulance. The doors were shut and the driver hurried round to the front of the vehicle.

"We'll take him to the infirmary," he called, as he jumped into the driver's seat and started the engine.

"I couldn't really make it out," Tessa replied, frowning slightly. "It sounded like 'poor' something – perhaps 'poor little' something."

"Poor little what?"

Tessa shrugged. "I couldn't hear," she explained, "but it was poor little *something*."

The policeman came over. "I'd like to take some statements from you two," he began, "but . . ." He looked up at the sky and then turned back to the two girls, "I don't think the weather's going to last out much longer."

Tessa and Sandy looked at each other. With all the rush and excitement, neither of them had noticed the weather, which had changed completely. Gone was the bright sunshine and the blue sky. Now, thick black clouds were competing with each other to darken the day as much as possible. The sun had disappeared completely and a chilly wind had sprung up.

"Perhaps . . ." said Tessa, as the first large drops of rain began to fall, "perhaps we should postpone our long ride . . ."

Rain lashed against the coffee-bar windows, but inside the room was warm and cheerful. Sue had made coffee, and now she could be seen in the indoor school, giving a dressage lesson.

"I'm glad we didn't go," Sandy admitted. She grinned at Tessa. "Tess the Pessimist was right, after all!"

"Of course!" Tessa agreed, modestly, as she unwrapped her lunch. "Oh well," she said, sighing, "this isn't by the stream on Burlington Down, but at least we're warm and dry."

Sandy delved into her haversack for her sandwiches. "The ponies would have hated it, too," she said.

The door from outside burst open and Adam stood on the mat. His hair clung wetly to his head and face, rain dripping from the ends and running down his nose and cheeks. His anorak and jodhpurs were dark with rain.

Tessa looked across at Sandy and winked. "Do you know," she said, languidly, "I think it might be raining!"

But the rain had not dampened Adam's spirits. He was grinning from ear to ear. His eyes lit on Tessa's sandwiches. He squelched over to her and stood, dripping, and looking at the food longingly.

"I'm starving!" he announced.

"Get off, you pig – I'm starving, too!" Tessa told him, bluntly.

"It's OK, Adam, you're saved if you've got cash," Sandy said, coming to Tessa's rescue. "Sue told me she'd made some sandwiches ready for this evening. They're in the kitchen, under a dish. They're 12p each. But tell her, won't you? She might need some more for the evening."

"There's coffee, too," Tessa called, as Adam made for the kitchen. "Sue said to help ourselves."

"Great." On his way over, Adam turned back. "She's come!" he announced, proudly.

"Cinnamon?"

"Yes. Cindy's here!"

"That's why you're looking so chuffed," said Tessa. "She's in the stable, is she?"

"Yes." Adam deposited his sandwiches and coffee on the table. "I'll be back in a minute," he added, "I'm going to change."

When Adam returned in dry clothes, the girls told him about their adventure.

"And was he all right – the old man?" Adam asked.

"We don't know," Tessa admitted.

"We've got to go to the police station to make statements," Sandy explained. Adam looked suitably impressed. "We still don't know what he was trying to say," she added. Adam wandered over to the window to see if the rain had eased.

A sudden understanding flickered in Tessa's eyes. She looked up quickly and spoke to Sandy. "I bet it was one of his animals," she said.

"Of course! You said he took on everyone's unwanted pets."

"Perhaps one of them is ill and he's worried about it," said Tessa.

"Oh Tess, we *must* go and see."

"We'll get soaked again," Tessa pointed out, "and I wanted to see Cindy."

"But it might be important!"

"OK, OK. Let me finish my sandwich!"

3

It had almost stopped raining by the time Tessa
and Sandy had fetched their bicycles from the
haybarn.

"It won't take long," Tessa said, as they splashed
through puddles on the cinder track leading from
the equestrian centre.

The two girls cycled along the lane, over the
motorway bridge and past a field of sheep. Turning towards Clereton, they were soon on their way
into the centre of town, leaving the old clock tower
to their right. Leading the way, Tessa took Sandy
past the big supermarket, with its piles of wire
baskets. Then, signalling left, she turned her bike
suddenly up a tiny, narrow lane, which Sandy had
not noticed before.

The lane led uphill, widening at the top to reveal
a row of small terraced cottages. Tessa stopped her
bike and propped it against the fence of the end
cottage.

"They're sweet – the cottages," Sandy said, leaving her bicycle next to Tessa's. "I didn't know there
were any houses up here."

"It's lovely, isn't it," Tessa agreed. She turned
and pointed back the way they had come. "The
views are great, across the moors, over the top of
the shops. Look! You can see Burlington Down in
the distance."

"And this is old Mr Crichley's cottage, is it?" Sandy asked, turning back. "He's got a bigger garden than the others."

"That's because it's the end one," Tessa pointed out. "Come on," she added, pushing open the garden gate, "let's investigate!"

The cottage garden was neat and well-tended. At the end were two wooden sheds, and a row of hutches of varying shapes, sizes and age. Tessa and Sandy peered in at the occupants – rabbits and guinea pigs.

"Well, they all look OK to me," Tessa stated. A half-grown black and white cat jumped up onto one of the hutches and rubbed up against her arm, purring loudly. Another cat – an old tortoiseshell – appeared and rubbed round Sandy's legs. The girls heard barking coming from the cottage, and turned to see a brown mongrel dog watching them from the window, his tail waving furiously as he barked.

"Quite a menagerie, isn't it?" said Tessa.

"Mm. They look well enough – but they'll need feeding," Sandy pointed out, "and the dog will want to be let out."

"I wonder —" Tessa began, but she was interrupted by a call from the next door garden.

"What are you up to? Don't you touch Mr Crichley's animals!"

A woman of about seventy was standing at the fence between Mr Crichley's front garden and the one next door, which was obviously hers. Her arms were folded squarely across her flowered apron.

The two girls looked at each other. "We'd better explain . . ." said Tessa.

"Oh dear, oh dear," said Mrs Loxton.

Tessa and Sandy, having told her about the accident, had been invited in to the next door cottage, and had been persuaded to have some tea and cake with the old woman, who told them that her name was Mrs Loxton.

"Poor Arthur," she moaned, wringing her hands.

"Don't worry, Mrs Loxton," Tessa said quickly. "He came round, and tried to speak to us. We think he's worried about one of his animals. Do you know if we can get into the cottage? Then we could take his dog for a walk and feed the animals for him."

"Well, of course, dears." Mrs Loxton seemed to have calmed down a little. "Arthur always leaves his back door open," she told them. "And those animals of his *will* need feeding, that's for sure," she added, shaking her head and tutting noisily. "I tell you what, my dears," she said, lowering her voice and leaning forward, conspiratorially, "he's a rum 'un, is Arthur Crichley."

"What do you mean, Mrs Loxton?" Tessa leaned forward too.

"Well . . . all these animals. And now –" Mrs Loxton lowered her voice even more, "– he's gone and got a *wild* one, I'm sure!"

"A wild animal?" Tessa looked at Sandy, and Sandy turned to look at the door. Her vivid imagination was already envisaging a lion padding down the passageway towards Mrs Loxton's kitchen.

"These past two nights," Mrs Loxton told them, her voice heavy with drama, "I've heard some very funny noises coming from his shed." She stopped and looked at her two listeners meaningfully.

"Funny noises?" Even down-to-earth Tessa was beginning to feel a shade uneasy.

Mrs Loxton shook her head. "Well, I never heard nothing like it – only when I went to the zoo when I were a nipper."

"I tell you what, Mrs Loxton," Sandy suggested, "perhaps we won't look inside the shed until – until we find out from Mr Crichley what's in it. Don't you think so, Tess?" she added, turning to her friend.

"I suppose that would be sensible," Tessa agreed. She pushed back her chair. "Well, thank you for the tea, Mrs Loxton – and the cake. We'll go and see to Mr Crichley's animals, now." She paused. "Er – which shed has got the wild animal in it?"

"The big one, my dear," Mrs Loxton replied. "All his tools are in the little one."

Emerging from the dimness of Mrs Loxton's narrow hallway, the girls found themselves blinking in bright sunshine. The storm clouds had rolled away, leaving a clear blue sky.

"Right!" said Tessa in her usual forthright manner. "To the jungle!"

"Don't!" Sandy exclaimed. "What do you think he's got in there, Tess? It can't *really* be a wild animal, can it?"

"Unless he found one – escaped from a zoo, or something."

"Er . . . let's go and see the dog."

"Good idea."

The brown mongrel, whose name Mrs Loxton

had told them was Monty, greeted them like long-lost friends.

"Poor little Monty," said Tessa extracting herself from his clambering paws and stroking his head while she looked about for a lead. "Did you think you'd been deserted?"

The two girls took Monty for a short walk down the lane and along the High Street as far as the football field. Then they brought him back to the cottage, gave him a couple of dog biscuits and some water, and promised to return in the evening to give him his supper and another walk.

Tessa found a cupboard containing old biscuit tins of rabbit and guinea-pig food, neatly labelled. The girls visited the row of hutches, filling up the empty pots and refilling the water bottles.

"We'll pick them some greenstuff from the moors, shall we?" Tessa said to Sandy. "We could bring it back this evening."

"And try not to get knocked down like poor old Mr Crichley," Sandy commented. "I wonder how he is?" she added.

"Mm. And I wonder what's in his shed!" Tessa edged closer to the wild animal shed. "It's got a little window at the back," she added, "I could just have a look . . ."

Cautiously, they walked a little nearer to the shed. Tessa, leading the way, looked in through the small, dirty window at the back of the wooden shed.

"It's a big shed, isn't it?" said Sandy, "You could get quite a large animal in there." She found herself whispering, and cleared her throat nervously.

Tessa rubbed at the grimy window and peered

in. "Can't see much," she announced. "It's so gloomy in there. Wait a minute," she added, "there's something . . ."

Involuntarily, Sandy stepped back a pace.

"I can't quite see," Tessa continued, flattening her nose against the glass. "It's so bright out here and so dark in there. There's something moving . . . two long things —"

The peace of the garden was suddenly broken by an ear-shattering, plaintive noise, sending the two girls leaping back in fright.

It went on and on; a foghorn of a noise, echoing round the small garden, and bouncing off the hutches. The rabbits and guinea-pigs stopped in mid-munch, turning startled eyes towards the shed.

At last, the sad, harsh, grating noise stopped. The two girls looked at each other. Laughter bubbled up inside Tessa and overflowed. "A wild animal!" she giggled. Sandy leaned against the shed and began to laugh, helplessly. "I thought . . ." She stopped to double up with laughter, "I thought, before, it might be a baby elephant!"

The two girls were stricken with laughter for a few minutes, and then they pulled themselves together.

"Do you really think," Tessa said at last, wiping the tears from her eyes, "that Mrs Loxton has never heard a donkey before?"

"I suppose not," Sandy replied. "After all, you can't mistake *that* noise! We'd better have a look," she added. "It must be miserable inside there – and perhaps *this* is the animal that Mr Crichley's worried about."

Purposefully, the two girls made for the door

of the shed. Pulling back the bolt, they opened the door, which echoed uneasily on its hinges.

The inside of the shed was dark, but clean. There was straw on the floor and a bucket of water in one corner. Next to the bucket was a makeshift manger – an old tea-chest which looked as if it had contained grass.

Turning his head to look at his visitors was the donkey. He was small, with a moth-eaten grey coat, and the saddest eyes that Sandy had ever seen.

"Oh . . ." All the laughter had gone, now, from Sandy's voice. "The poor little thing," she breathed.

The donkey was painfully thin. Even under the thick, matted coat, his small frame was sharp and angular. Large, forlorn eyes stared at the two girls from a head which seemed too large for such a thin body. He stood, awkwardly, in the straw, with feet which had obviously been left untrimmed for a long time, and had grown and curved upwards at the front, looking a little like Dutch clogs.

Tessa's voice, when she spoke, was angry.

"I thought old Mr Crichley *liked* animals," she said tersely. "How *could* he treat one like this?"

4

"In you jump, then!"

Police Constable Thrower held open the door, and Tessa and Sandy found themselves inside a police car for the first time in their lives.

"I feel a bit . . . sort of criminal," Sandy whispered.

"It's just an ordinary car," Tessa pointed out, leaning back against the seat. "It's not as if they're rushing us off with flashing lights, or anything."

"Hey!" Sandy had a sudden thought. "Do you think we ought to tell the mothers? After all, they think we're on Burlington Down."

"Mm. P'raps you're right," Tessa agreed.

So there were a couple of slight diversions, while the two mothers were visited and the day's events related quickly. Then the girls sat back while they were transported to the infirmary.

After seeing Mr Crichley's animals, Tessa and Sandy had visited the police station to give their statements. P. C. Thrower had told them that he would be interviewing Mr Crichley later that afternoon, and Tessa had begged a lift.

"What are you going to say to him?" Sandy asked her friend, in a whisper, as they sped through the country lanes towards the city. "You can't very well grumble at the poor old man – he's ill in hospital!"

"I don't know," Tessa admitted. "Let's just see how he is, first."

With the two policemen striding ahead, Tessa and Sandy were ushered quickly through the wide, disinfectant-smelling corridors of the infirmary to a small room just off the emergency unit. There, pale-faced and fragile-looking, lay old Mr Crichley, propped up on his pillows, his head bandaged and two plasters on his face.

"He's a very lucky old man," said the sister, pausing just outside the door. "Apart from the shock, the only real damage was a nasty gash on his head and two cracked ribs."

"Can he remember anything?" asked P. C. Thrower.

The sister chuckled. "Oh yes!" she said. "He can remember about the accident – and plenty more besides! He's a canny one, is old Mr Crichley. He keeps on and on about his animals."

The two girls looked at each other.

"Will it be all right if I ask him a few questions?" asked the policeman.

"Yes, you go ahead," the sister replied. "I've got to check the main ward. I'll leave you to it." She turned penetrating eyes upon the two girls. "Are they with you?" she added, a little suspiciously.

"Yes. They've come with us. They found him and called for the ambulance."

The sister nodded briefly and was gone, striding purposefully away down the corridor.

The two policemen seemed to fill the small

room. Tessa and Sandy hovered near the door, as P. C. Thrower began.

"Now, Mr Crichley, we don't want to tire you, but we'd like to ask you a few questions . . ."

The girls listened, while Mr Crichley's old but surprisingly strong voice told of the car which had thrown him into the ditch.

"I turned me head, just at the last minute," he told the policemen, "and all I can tell you is that the car was red. Then it hit me. And then I remember seein' you." He peered round the two men, "and those two girls, there – and their ponies. I see'd 'em yesterday, too."

P. C. Thrower asked a few more questions. Then he said, "I'll just write out my notes, Mr Crichley, and then we'll leave you in peace."

"Well now," said the old man, "there's a table and chairs just outside in the corridor. I can see them through the glass. You'll be able to do your writing there." He smiled up at them, benignly.

As the two policemen turned towards the door, old Mr Crichley looked at the two girls. He lifted a hand and beckoned to them, furtively, turning back to watch the policemen uneasily. When they had gone, he spoke in an anxious whisper.

"Quick! While they're out o' the way. I want to speak to you!"

Sandy and Tessa moved to the bedside. "We want to speak to you, too," Tessa said.

"First of all," said old Mr Crichley, "thank 'ee kindly for saving me life. I'd ha' been a gonner, but for you two girls."

"That's all right," said Sandy, "but we want to talk —"

"The other thing," said the old man, lowering his voice even further, "is my animals. They need looking after – I'm so worried about them —"

"Don't worry, Mr Crichley," Tessa broke in. "We're seeing to your animals. But we want to talk to you about the donkey —"

The old man's faded blue eyes lit up. Now it was his turn to interrupt. "You've seen 'im, have you – my poor little Cecil?"

Tessa looked at Sandy and she couldn't resist a smile. Cecil didn't sound a very likely name for a donkey. However ... "Yes, we have," she told him, "and —"

"Poor little Cecil," the old man repeated. "We've got to do something about him." He looked furtively towards the two policemen, who were still bent over their notepads. "The vet's coming to see him," he continued, in a whisper. "I arranged it yesterday. He's coming in the morning – nine o'clock. And Ted Halliwell's coming at eleven o'clock to cut Cecil's feet."

"But Mr Crichley, why did you let Cecil get into this state?" Tessa looked perplexed.

"I didn't," the old man replied, indignantly. "Someone else did!"

"But —"

"That's why I don't want *them* to know," the old man continued, casting an anxious glance in the policemen's direction. "You see ..." His voice sunk even lower, so that the girls had to bend down close to hear him. "You see ... I *stole* 'im!"

"That's right," said Adam, "Dad's going to see his

donkey in the morning. He told me about it. The old man wanted him to go urgently, but tomorrow morning was the first time Dad could manage."

The three of them were in the tack room. Adam had been for his first ride on Cindy, and was putting the saddle and bridle away when Tessa and Sandy had questioned him about the donkey.

Sandy looked at Tessa. "We'll tell Adam, won't we?"

"I think so," Tessa replied. "You can keep a secret, can't you, Adam?"

"Of *course* I can," Adam replied, indignantly. "What's up?"

"The donkey your Dad's going to see," Sandy explained, "it's stolen!"

"Wow!" Adam ran his fingers through his thick fringe of hair.

"But it's not as bad as it sounds," Tessa put in, hastily. "It's all in a good cause!"

"Old Mr Crichley found it, you see, in a terrible state." Sandy took up the tale. "It was tethered on this bit of rough ground, with just a short rope —"

"And no water," Tessa interrupted.

"And it was terribly thin," Sandy continued, "and its feet were in a very bad state. Old Mr Crichley tried to find out who owned it, but nobody knew. He took it some water and grass, and he gave it some extra rope."

"But he couldn't keep travelling over there," said Tessa, "and he was so angry with whoever it is who owns it that he went over late Tuesday evening —"

"And he stole it!" Sandy finished the story, triumphantly.

"Good for him!" cried Adam. "But —" The two girls looked anxious. "I think old Mr Crichley's in the clear, anyway," Adam stated.

"How do you mean?" asked Tessa.

"Well, I'm sure Dad told me about a new ruling for tethering. I *think* whoever owns that donkey may have been breaking the law."

"And so old Mr Crichley might not be in trouble, after all?"

"Well, I would think the police would be more interested in speaking to the owner about the donkey than to old Mr Crichley."

"So what do you think we should do, Adam?" Tessa asked.

"Perhaps you should tell the police and then maybe they can find the owner."

"Well, it may not be as easy as all that."

Tessa and Sandy had managed to catch P. C. Thrower before he went off duty. The policeman rubbed his chin, thoughtfully. "You see," he told them, "no one has reported a lost donkey – and you'd think they would, straight away, wouldn't you? I think," he continued, not waiting for an answer to his question, "that whoever owns that donkey *knows* they've been breaking the law and we shan't hear from them. And trying to find the owner will be difficult by the sound of it."

"Unfortunately," he added, chuckling at his own joke, "donkeys don't have number plates and log books!"

"But what can we do with him?" Tessa said. "I mean – he can't really stay in that shed for long. That would be almost as cruel as tethering him badly."

"Mm . . ." P. C. Thrower rubbed his chin again. "We could ask the RSPCA," he said. "In fact, I must do. But I know they're chock-a-block just now. It's summer holiday time, you see, and some people just turn their animals out when they go on holiday."

"People are horrible!" Tessa said, vehemently.

"Mostly just thoughtless," the policeman said placidly. "If the donkey's in as bad a state as you say," he continued, "then the RSPCA might recommend that he's put down —"

"No! Not poor little Cecil!"

"I'm afraid so."

"But we'll let the vet look at him first, won't we?" said Tessa quickly.

"And if the vet says Cecil will be all right with some care . . ." Sandy put it.

"And if we can find him a field . . ."

"Yes . . . well," P. C. Thrower edged towards the door, thinking of his long-awaited supper. "Let's just see how we get on, shall we?"

5

"I thought we'd never get out on the ponies again!" Tessa spoke from Duskie's back.

"Me, too," agreed Sandy, as she jumped up into Quest's saddle. The lively chestnut chewed on her snaffle bit and shook her head, impatiently, but she stood still while Sandy mounted.

"Good girl, you're improving," Sandy told her, patting her. Quest had been in the habit of moving off before her rider had settled properly into the saddle, and Sandy had been trying to correct her.

The girls had spent a busy morning tending to Mr Crichley's animals and dealing with the blacksmith and Mr Maiyer, the vet. Now they were back at the equestrian centre, ready for a ride.

"Hi!"

As the girls set off from the yard, a voice hailed them, accompanied by the clatter of trotting hooves.

Sandy and Tessa reined in their ponies as Kate, a girl of seventeen, trotted up beside them. She was riding her 15.2 part-thoroughbred gelding.

"Hi!" Kate said again, breathlessly. She slowed her horse to a walk as the two girls set off again. "Can I come with you?"

"Great!" Tessa agreed. "We're only going for a shortish ride, to the tracks on the moors."

"That'll suit me fine," Kate said, settling in beside

them as they walked down the cinder path towards the lane.

Costa, her horse, which she kept at Heronsway, strode out with his easy, long stride. He was a strongly built twelve-year-old bright bay, with a calm, amiable disposition.

"I've got an interview this afternoon at the fruit farm," Kate told her companions chattily. "It's down that lane, on the hill, near the motorway." She pointed to a lane leading off the one which the cinder path joined. "But I'll have to get home first to change." She grinned. "Can't go for an interview smelling of horses!" she added.

At the end of the cinder path they met Adam, who was returning from a ride on Cindy.

"At last I've seen Cindy!" said Tessa. "What's she like to ride?"

"Brilliant!" Adam replied. "But you saw her at the three-day event," he reminded her.

"Yes, but that was with that Fiona girl riding her!"

"How did Dad get on with the donkey?" Adam asked, turning his pony round to walk alongside the others.

As they continued down the lane, Sandy told Adam about the vitamin injection which Adam's father had given Cecil, and about the special instructions which he had left. "We have to give him very small amounts of bran mash," she explained, "with molasses in it."

"What he needs now is some proper grazing," Tessa said, as they reached the first track. "That's what your dad said Cecil needs — as well as the food, of course."

Adam laughed. "Whatever made the old man call him Cecil?" he asked.

"He said he used to have a friend, years ago, called Cecil," Tessa explained, "and this friend had an expression just like the donkey's – very mournful, with soulful brown eyes! Poor little Cecil," she added, seriously. "It would be lovely to see him looking well again. He looks so pathetic."

"Well, at least Mr Maiyer doesn't think he needs to be put down," Sandy reminded her.

Kate was still thinking about the grazing problem. "Perhaps Sue and Peter would let you keep him at the centre – just for a while," she suggested.

"What do you think, Chrissy?"

Tessa had managed to stop Chrissy Baker in mid-flight between the stable-block and the indoor school. Seventeen-year-old Chrissy was a pupil at the equestrian centre, working and learning, while she waited to hear the results of her Assistant Instructor's examinations, which she had taken recently. Hard-working Chrissy was always in a hurry, and it was sometimes quite difficult to catch her.

"About this donkey, you mean?" Chrissy, who had paused with a large wooden mallet in one hand, was actually standing still for a moment. However, she looked as though she would be setting off again at any moment. "I don't really know," she admitted, running the fingers of her free hand through her short dark hair agitatedly, and frowning slightly as she thought. "It's difficult, you see," she said to the two girls. "Peter and Sue are *so* rushed just now. This afternoon there's a jumping competition in the indoor school and a dressage event outside. Then this evening they've got some television people coming to see them. They want to televise a programme here later on, apparently. And, of course, the gymkhana's looming!"

"So you don't think I can bother them by asking about grazing for the donkey?" Tessa asked.

"Sue seems so worn out just now," Chrissy explained. "I'll tell you what," she said, seeing their crestfallen faces, "I'll ask Peter when there's a lull." She grinned at them as she set off towards the indoor school, the mallet over her shoulder. "Keep up the donkey-saving work!" she called, disappearing at a brisk run.

Having eaten their packed lunch in Duskie's stable, planning their postponed ride to Burlington Down, Sandy and Tessa spent the next hour pulling grass from the roadside for Cecil, and packing it into plastic bags.

They worked in dedicated silence for a while. Then Tessa sat back on her heels for a rest. "And *I* thought these holidays would be one long series of rides on Duskie," she said ruefully. "Just shows how wrong you can be."

"We'll get out on our long ride," Sandy assured her. "I'm sure we will. What about tomorrow?"

"We ought to wait," Tessa replied, "until Mr Maiyer has been again. I mean, we *are* supposed to be feeding Cecil regularly throughout the day. We're a bit late now with his next feed."

"Mm. Yes, of course, I'd forgotten," Sandy admitted. "Oh well," she added, tearing at the grass with renewed vigour, "p'raps when Mr Maiyer has been again – he said he'd come on Monday, didn't he?" Tessa nodded. "And if we can get some grazing for Cecil," Sandy continued, "we'll go on Tuesday, shall we? I'm sure Mrs Loxton will let Monty out at lunchtime."

"Great!" Tessa agreed. "We won't let anything stop us!"

"It's OK!" Chrissy called that evening, looking out from one of the stables. She was busy bedding down the last of her charges before leaving for her evening job at a local pub. Chrissy hoped, one day, to be able to buy Merlin, the pony which she rode at the centre. Merlin belonged to Sue and Peter, and Chrissy had arranged that she would buy Merlin when she had saved enough money. But money was tight in Chrissy's family, and most of her pub earnings went to pay the family bills.

"I've arranged it for you," Chrissy said, when the two girls came over. "Peter said you can put the donkey in that little orchard by the caravan – you know, where they keep their hens." She slapped the big black gelding affectionately on the quarters, before letting herself out and closing up the stable for the night. "He said you can put him out in the big jumping field next to it, when there's no eventing taking place. But put him back in the orchard at night, anyway. And of course," she added, walking back towards the side of the tack room, where she kept her motor-scooter, "you'll have to keep him well and truly in the orchard next week, when the gymkhana's on!"

"Thanks, Chrissy – that's great!" said Sandy.

"We're going to leave him in his shed until Monday, anyway," Tessa told her. "Adam's dad's going to have another look at him then, and give him another injection."

"I'm sure he looked better this afternoon," Sandy said. "We took him loads of grass and gave him his food."

"And we're pinching some of Duskie's hay for him this evening."

"Good. I'm glad that's sorted out," Chrissy said. "Incidentally," she added, "I'm not sure that you should give donkeys hay. I think I read somewhere that they eat straw. Better ask Mr Maiyer. I must dash now." Chrissy smiled at them, but her eyes were worried, Sandy noticed. Was there something wrong, she wondered?

6

Sunday began like any other Sunday at Heronsway. Tessa and Sandy mucked out the ponies' stables in the early morning, as usual. Chrissy, busy with the livery horses, waved to them from one of the stables.

"I wonder when Sarah and Andrea are back?" Tessa said, when the two friends met at their usual rendezvous by the muck-heap.

"Sometime today, I think," Sandy replied.

Sarah, a quiet, shy thirteen-year-old, and twelve-year-old Andrea had been away together for a week's holiday at a trekking centre, with their own ponies, Puffin and Ragamuffin. Since riding at Heronsway, and taking part in the successful team competing for the three-day event cup, Sarah had come out of her shell considerably. Andrea, a spoilt only child, had been difficult and sullen until Sandy had caught her tampering with Quest, and had shamed her into becoming a more thoughtful member of the Heronsway "regulars". Andrea had felt unwanted and unliked by the others, but since helping the team to win the cup, and with some encouragement from Sandy, she had become a much more competent rider and happier altogether.

"They seem quite good friends now," Tessa remarked, picking up the handles of her wheelbarrow.

"Mm. Do them both good," Sandy remarked.

The girls had decided to take their ponies with them, this time, when they went up to Hunter's Lane to see Mr Crichley's animals and Cecil.

"We'll leave the headcollars on, shall we?" Sandy suggested. "Then we can tie them up to the gate."

"Good idea," Tessa agreed.

Adam, who had arrived earlier and had disappeared into Cindy's stable with the radiant glow of new ownership on his face, now emerged, leading his pony. Cindy, a bay mare of 14.2 hands, was a lovely pony. Despite her previous treatment, she had a quiet and calm temperament. Adam patted her and then mounted and adjusted his stirrups.

"I still can't quite decide what length to have them," he told the girls. "What do you think?" he asked. "Does that look right? I've put them up a hole."

Tessa stared, critically. "Looks about right to me," she declared at last. "Don't you think?" she asked Sandy.

"Spot on!" Sandy declared, without hesitation. "I've just been reading in one of the horse magazines that Mum stocks that people often have their stirrups too long," she added.

"I suppose you don't have to buy your own magazines," Adam said.

"Not if I'm careful when I read them," Sandy replied, with a grin.

"All right for some!" Tessa commented, gathering up her reins and mounting Duskie.

"Are you going out for a long ride?" Adam

asked, eyeing the headcollars. The girls explained. "I'd like to see Cecil," he admitted.

"The more the merrier!" Tessa said.

Cecil was pleased to see them. Peering from the gloom of his shed, he brayed his wild animal greeting. Then he stood looking at them hopefully, from his big, soulful brown eyes, below long fine lashes.

"I know it's only two days, but he really *does* look better, I'm sure," Sandy said, putting an arm around the donkey's grey neck. But she shuddered, nevertheless, when she felt the nearness of Cecil's bones beneath the tangled grey coat.

Sandy inspected the makeshift manger. "He's finished his grass and food," she reported.

"Poor old lad." Adam ran his hands down one of Cecil's legs and inspected the small hoof. "Were his feet very bad?" he asked.

"Bad enough," Tessa replied.

"I'll let him feed on the lawn," Sandy said, leading the donkey carefully from the shed. "It's your turn to clean out the shed," she informed Tessa.

"We don't like to tether him, you see," Tessa explained to Adam, picking up the garden spade. "We think he must have *hated* it."

"I'll help." Adam looked around for more tools.

"Only garden tools, I'm afraid," Tessa told him. She nodded towards the back of the shed. "Wheelbarrow's there. And a garden rake and an almost bald brush. Not exactly all mod cons at old Mr Crichley's!"

Just over an hour later, when all the animals had been fed and cleaned out, and Monty had been given his morning walk to the football field, the three were able to remount their somewhat bored ponies. Quest had begun to paw the ground restlessly, whilst Duskie had rested one hind leg and closed his eyes, leaning his head against the top of the gate.

"You dozy old thing, Duskie!" Tessa declared, waking him up as she lifted the saddle flap and tightened the girth.

Quest whickered as Sandy approached. "I hope Cindy gets to know me like that soon," Adam said, smoothing his pony's neck. Cindy nuzzled him gently.

"Tell you what!" Tessa looked at the other two. "Now we're here, in Clereton, why don't we go on past the football field and up through the woods to the camp?"

"Have a longish ride after all? Great!" said Sandy. "We could ask Mrs Loxton to let Monty out at lunchtime."

"Then if we went along the top and past the camp, we could come down that bridleway to Thelham and ride back to Heronsway across the moors!" Adam put in triumphantly.

This plan was universally agreed and the three ponies and riders set off down the High Street towards the eastern end of the town.

After riding up a winding path through steep woodland, the riders dismounted and led their ponies across a footbridge which spanned the motorway. The narrow bridge, high above the road, with its rushing streams of traffic below, led to a wide path. This path ran for several miles along a hilly ridge, at the end of which was the old Roman camp.

In places the path along the ridge was stony, but some parts were soft and grassy. Here, the riders urged their ponies to a fast canter. Sandy had never been on this ride before. It felt, she thought, as though she and Quest were cantering along the top of the world. Below them, to the left, she saw glimpses of a wide valley, and to their right lay the Clere Moors. Flat and peaceful, the moors were criss-crossed with ditches, and the friendly little River Clere wound its way through the fields.

At the Roman camp, which was fenced off, the three turned their ponies towards the bridlepath which led down to the road. At Thelham, they took the lane which led across the moors, and the ponies walked and jogged towards the centre.

"I'm starving!" Adam announced, "I'm so hungry, I could eat a —"

"No you couldn't!" Sandy told him quickly.

"You're always hungry," Tessa said.

"We've been ages," Adam protested.

"It's a lovely ride," Sandy said. "We must go on more long rides this holiday."

"Don't forget Tuesday," Tessa reminded her, "Burlington Down!" She turned to Adam. "Can you come?" she asked him. "It's a brilliant ride." She grinned. "We'll take a packed lunch," she added.

"Great! You bet I will!"

But it was a long time before the three of them did get out for their long ride . . .

As they came to the more familiar stretch of the moorland road, past the old stone bridge and the pollarded willows, the ponies swung along at a slightly faster walk, their heads up and ears pricked.

"Duskie's imagining that bucket," said Tessa.

"Mm. Food. Sounds a good idea," Adam said, enthusiastically.

"Look!" Sandy pointed. "That might be Sarah and Andrea."

Sandy's finger was pointing in the direction of the equestrian centre, where a horsebox trundled slowly down the cinder path.

By the time the three ponies had reached the path, the horsebox was in the car park, disgorging its load. First Puffin, a dapple-grey pony, was led down the ramp followed by Rags, a pretty skewbald. The two ponies stood gazing about them. Sarah, holding Puffin by his headcollar, waved excitedly.

"Hi!" she called as the others came nearer. "We're back!"

But the three riders ignored her completely. They had halted their ponies and were staring towards the far end of the indoor school.

Sarah had her back to the school. "What's the matter?" she asked, and as she spoke both she and Andrea swung round to look.

The huge sliding door which led to the indoor school was open, and parked in the doorway was an ambulance. As the five watched in silence, a stretcher was lifted in. Peter scrambled in after it, the doors were closed, and the ambulance drove off, carefully but speedily around the exercise area and down the cinder path, swiftly passing the five watchers.

7

They arrived at the entrance to the indoor school, where Chrissy stood, looking pale and shocked.

"What's happened?" Tessa asked urgently. "Did someone fall off?"

Chrissy shook her head. "It's Sue," she said, her voice shaky.

"Is she hurt?" Sandy asked.

Chrissy looked up. The worry that Sandy had seen earlier in her eyes had now taken over Chrissy's face. "Not *hurt*," she said, slowly, "she's ill. She hasn't seemed well for ages. She collapsed. It's awful."

"What —" Adam began, but was interrupted by a voice from the indoor school.

"I say – Miss!" The voice was friendly, if just a little peeved.

"Mrs Mountford! I'd forgotten you were there." Chrissy looked startled.

"Shall I leave it for now?" the voice asked. "Sultan and I just started our lesson when Mr Venables had to leave. I'm sorry about Mrs Venables. I hope she'll be all right. Perhaps we should forget our lesson for today?" Instead of being just a disembodied voice, Mrs Mountford appeared, walking her horse out of the school. Sultan, big, black and powerful, stood in the sunlight, with Mrs Mountford, a small, middle-aged, slightly anxious-looking woman, perched on his back.

For a moment, Chrissy hesitated. She looked at the others and then back at Mrs Mountford.

"No – no, Mrs Mountford. You go back in. I'll be there in two ticks!"

Looking pleased, Mrs Mountford turned Sultan back into the indoor school. Chrissy looked up at the rest of them. "Can one of you man the kitchen?" she asked, quickly. "And someone answer the telephone? Warrior and Mickie need exercising." There was a light of determination in her eyes. "Let's keep it going until Peter comes back!"

It was nearly nine o'clock before they all met up again in the coffee-bar lounge. The five younger riders had telephoned home to explain, and then had set to work. There had been lessons throughout the late afternoon and evening, taken by Chrissy. Meanwhile, having put their own ponies into their stables, the others had taken over the various duties normally undertaken by Chrissy. Thirty-five horses and ponies had to be fed and bedded down and two of them exercised.

Kate, who had come in later on, took over the kitchen and the office, dividing her time between brewing coffee and frying chips for the clients who had come for their lessons, and answering the telephone in the office.

"They seem to have such rapacious appetites after they've had a lesson," she remarked to Chrissy. "I've booked in more lessons for next week," she added when, at last, they were all able to sit down.

"That's OK," Chrissy answered her. "Peter'll be back."

"I've never worked so hard in my life!" Adam spoke from one of the armchairs, where he lay in a collapsed state.

Tessa yawned from another chair. "I'm *so* tired!" she said. A chorus of yawns indicated that the others were feeling the same.

The last of the riders who had had a lesson poked his head around the door.

"Cheerio, all!" he called. "Can't stop for coffee tonight. Hope everything goes well with Mrs Venables. Great lesson!" he added to Chrissy, before leaving.

"I really think I'll have to go," Sandy said, "or else I'll fall asleep here. And –" she looked across at Tessa, "we've got Mr Crichley's animals to do!"

Tessa groaned. "I'd forgotten about them," she admitted.

"I'll help," said Adam.

"Mr Crichley's animals?" Andrea echoed. She and Sarah looked mystified.

"We'll have to tell you tomorrow," said Sandy, heaving herself reluctantly from her chair. As she spoke, the telephone rang.

"A bit late," Kate grumbled, but she hurried to answer it. When she came back into the room, her face was serious. "It was Peter," she said. "They think Sue's got meningitis. She's very ill. Peter's staying with her, and he won't be back tonight."

No one spoke. At last, Chrissy broke the silence.

"Well," she said, her voice determined. "All *we* can do is keep the centre going. How about it, team?"

Chrissy stayed the night at the centre. "I can't just *leave* it," she explained to the others. "There are the horses and the hens – and Freddie!"

Freddie, Peter and Sue's large black mongrel puppy, had slept through the drama of the day and had emerged during the evening, to pester Kate for food in the kitchen. Freddie, at the gangly, teenage, all-legs stage of his young life, rested two large front paws on Chrissy's knee and snuffled noisily in her ear until she extracted herself from her comfortable chair to forage for dog food.

"I'll be OK," she assured the others, as they prepared to leave. "There's a spare bed space in the caravan, and I know where the sleeping bags are. I'll leave a message at the hospital to tell Peter what I'm doing. Freddie and I will keep each other company – and I won't have far to travel to work!"

The next morning Tessa and Sandy made a brief early morning visit to the centre to muck out their ponies. While they were there, Adam, Sarah and Andrea arrived. Kate had started work at the fruit farm that morning.

"See you later, Chrissy." Tessa looked over Captain's stable door. Captain was trotting round the exercise area, snorting into the soft morning air, while Chrissy cleaned out his stable.

"It's donkey day," Sandy reminded her, joining Tessa at the stable door. "I hope it'll still be all right."

Chrissy straightened up. "Of course! Cecil's coming to stay!" she said delightedly. "He'll be no trouble, I'm sure."

Despite the early hour, Mrs Loxton was waiting at her garden gate, bursting with news.

"They're sending him home on Friday," she told the two girls, as soon as they were within earshot. "Daft, I call it."

"I expect he'll be glad to be home," Sandy pointed out, but Mrs Loxton only sniffed non-committally.

Mr Maiyer arrived promptly at eight thirty, and pronounced Cecil much improved.

"Some good grass will work wonders now, I reckon," he said. He turned to the two girls approvingly. "You've done well," he told them. "Luckily, old Mr Crichley caught Cecil before his health had deteriorated too badly." He looked at them with serious brown eyes, like his son's. "You'll have to think of a permanent home for Cecil before too long," he told them. "Still," he added, packing up his case and snapping the lid shut, "it sounds as though you've got your work cut out, just now, all of you. Adam told me about Mrs Venables," he said. "I think you're all doing a grand job." He turned to go, and then stopped. "I'm pretty busy just now, myself," he told them, "but if there's anything I can do to help —"

Tessa, never afraid to jump in, feet first, said quickly, "There's the gymkhana on Saturday – we thought we'd ask parents to help. I don't suppose you'd be our official vet?"

After Mr Crichley's animals had been fed, and Monty taken for a walk, the girls turned to the next job of the day.

"Come on, Cecil," said Tessa, undoing the head-collar rope. "Time for walkies!" But Cecil could see no reason to leave his food. Planting his feet firmly, he resisted Tessa's tugs.

"Perhaps if I bring it . . ." Sandy picked up the bucket of food and walked towards the gate. Seeing the best thing in his life disappearing down the garden path, Cecil swung round, nearly pulling Tessa off her feet.

"Cecil!" Tessa gasped, trotting along beside him. "I didn't know you could move so fast!"

At the equestrian centre, Cecil greeted the orchard with enthusiasm. Ignoring all around him, he put his head down and tore at the grass greedily. The hens, who ran to inspect this intruder into their territory, followed him round for a while, clucking in shocked tones, but soon lost interest and returned to their pecking.

"We'd better report for duty," Sandy said, adding with a grin, "I'll give you three guesses at what we're to be doing for the next hour or so!"

Chrissy called a meeting at lunchtime.

"I rang through to the hospital," she told the others. "No good news, I'm afraid. Sue's in this sort of . . . coma. Peter won't leave her." She looked round at them all, anxiously. "You all want to do it, don't you?" she asked. "Keep it going here, I mean? It's all we can do, isn't it?" There was a chorus of assent, and Chrissy looked relieved. "I knew I could rely on the Heronsway team!" she said, grinning. Then, leaning forward, Chrissy continued. "I've been looking at Sue's plans for the gymkhana

– and really it's all done! Everything's arranged and ordered. You know how efficient Sue is." She stopped. "We can cope, can't we, on Saturday? It'll be a piece of cake!"

The others looked round at each other. It seemed quite an undertaking, to run a horse show and gymkhana.

Adam was spokesman. "Shouldn't we all have particular jobs for Saturday?" he asked Chrissy.

"Yes. Well, I've made a list," Chrissy laid out Sue's plan of the show on one of the tables and everyone gathered round.

"Sue's got two rings, you see – one for showing classes and one for jumping. And then the big field will be for the gymkhana events, the clear-round jumping and the stalls."

"Stalls?" Tessa echoed.

"Mm. The tack shop in Thelham – they're having a sort of small marquee. And the corn stores from Portersbury. And we'll be running a hot dog stand."

"What about judges?" Sarah asked.

"It's all organized," Chrissy assured them. "Sue's even arranged for outside caterers for the judges' lunches." She grinned at them. "I'm afraid we'll have to make do with the hot dogs, though! Now then," she continued briskly, picking up her pen, "there will be seven of us. And I've got jobs for at least sixteen. We're going to have to enlist parents. Any offers?"

"I couldn't offer *you*, could I, Mum?" Not waiting for a reply, Sandy continued, "Besides, we're just about all right – though Chrissy's not too sure about her father."

"Mmm ..." Mrs Corfield, only listening with half an ear, was sitting at the dining-room table, frowning over the shop accounts.

Sandy put her feet up and lay along the shabby old sofa which took up almost the entire wall of the small living room. Also packed into the room was the dining table and chairs, an oak sideboard, a small coffee table and a standard lamp. This was the room where Sandy and her mother lived, ate and talked. The kitchen was very small, and the other room downstairs had been taken over by stock for the sweet and newspaper shop which Sandy's mother worked. Sandy's parents had separated, deciding, quite amicably, to divorce, and Dad now lived in a flat in London.

Giving up the idea of talking, since Mum seemed to be preoccupied and Sandy was tired, anyway, after a day of mucking out stables and exercising the livery horses, she allowed her mind to wander to Quest.

With everything seeming to happen at once, right at the start of the holidays – Mr Crichley's animals and Cecil, and now Sue's illness and the forthcoming gymkhana – Sandy had almost forgotten that Quest was her own pony for the next year. Quest, the beautiful chestnut pony, with her brown eyes which were sometimes soft and dreamy, sometimes mischievous; Quest, with her long fine mane and tail, and her lovely chestnut head which she held so proudly. Sandy reached up to stroke the pony's soft neck . . .

"Sandy!"

Sandy jerked awake, to see Mum looking at her over her glasses.

"Why don't you try bed?" Mum suggested. "I'm sure it's more comfortable than that old sofa. You can take Boxer up with you."

Sandy looked down to find herself stroking her tabby cat, not Quest's sleek chestnut neck!

"Right." Sandy gathered Boxer into her arms. "I tell you one thing, Mum," she yawned, "I'm an expert, now, at mucking out stables!"

"Hmp! Pity you're not an expert at mucking out bedrooms!"

There was really no answer to that, Sandy decided, and made her way to bed hastily, before Mum had any more thoughts on the subject!

8

As the week continued, with warm sunny weather setting in, the Heronsway workers settled down to a routine of sorts. With Kate away at work during the day, Andrea turned out to be the most efficient in the office.

"She's amazing on the phone," Chrissy told Tessa, during a brief interlude between lessons. "She's much more positive and friendly than she used to be."

Since the kitchen was next door to the office, Andrea also became chief cook and coffee maker, trotting backwards and forwards between making sandwiches in readiness for the evening, and answering the telephone to book in lessons and entries for competitions.

Adam and the three girls continued with the ever-present mucking-out routine, leaving Chrissy free to give lessons and to exercise the larger livery horses.

"Won't it be great to have just one pony to muck out again?" Adam leaned back against a bale of straw as he spoke. The four stable workers were taking a quick break in the feed room.

"Unbelievable!" Tessa agreed.

"I've been thinking," Adam continued, slowly, looking out of the open door at the blue sky.

"Careful! You might do some damage!" said

Tessa.

Adam threw a handful of straw in her direction, before continuing. "The weather's perfect for camping." The others looked at him expectantly, as he paused. "So why don't we?" he finished.

"Here – at Heronsway, you mean?" asked Sandy.

"We'd have to ask Peter," Sarah pointed out.

"I haven't got a tent," said Sandy.

"Mine's big enough for two," Tessa told her. Turning to Adam, she added, "It *would* be fun. We could camp in the orchard."

It was Wednesday. There had been a rush that morning since Ted Halliwell, the blacksmith, had arrived at eight thirty to shoe five of the livery horses. Ted, a burly, kind-hearted man in his mid-forties, with a genuine love of the horses that he shod, enquired after Cecil, so Sandy rode Quest to fetch Cecil from his orchard. It had been discovered that Cecil *loved* horses, Quest in particular, whom he would follow anywhere.

Ted Halliwell put down his rasp and straightened up when Cecil arrived.

"Well now," he said, wiping the sweat from his forehead with a practised hand, "that's a much happier looking donkey than the one I saw last Saturday. Looks quite perky now."

Cecil was pushing out his grey nose to blow through his nostrils at the sixteen hand bay horse, Captain, that Ted Halliwell was shoeing. The girls had told Ted Cecil's history. "Reckon you'll have to find a home for him afore winter," he said.

Before bending to pick up Captain's foot again, he added. "One o' them special homes might take him on."

Sandy looked thoughtful as she rode Quest back to the orchard, with Cecil following. Why hadn't she thought of Aunt Cress before, she wondered. That evening, she would write a letter.

In the late afternoon, while Chrissy finished her last lesson of the day in the exercise area, the others began to assemble the jumps in the indoor school. An unaffiliated jumping competition was due to be held there that evening.

Andrea produced Sue's jumping plan.

"There are ten actual jumps," she said, "including the double. Two down that side —" she pointed across the school "— and three this side, the wall and the double."

"Let's see." Adam looked over her shoulder. "Oh yes, I remember," he said, peering at the paper, "the others are angled down the centre of the school. I entered last time," he told her, "but I didn't get anywhere. Of course," he added, "I didn't have Cindy then!"

"Are you going to enter this evening?" Tessa asked him. She, too, had stopped to view the plan.

"We'll be too busy organizing, won't we?" Adam asked.

"I don't see why," Tessa replied. "Sue and Peter manage, usually, with a couple of helpers — and someone in the kitchen, of course. And we can't open the bar — we're not old enough. There are

59

seven of us, after all. You have a go, Adam – see how Cindy does."

Adam pushed back his fringe excitedly. "I'd like to," he admitted.

"We've had a lot of entries," Andrea told him.

Tessa turned to Andrea. "Has that horrible man entered?" she asked her. "Derek something?"

"Derek Bute do you mean? Yes, he has."

"Mmm. That's the one. Bute the Brute, Sue calls him," Tessa said. "He's so rough with his horse. She's lovely, too – very young. Peter says he'll *ruin* her."

"The trouble is," Chrissy contributed, having finished her lesson and joined the others in the indoor school, "he usually wins the competition. Cracker is a really smashing jumper. If Bute the Brute would just stop winding her up with his shouting and his terrible riding, she would go on to do really well. That's what Peter says, anyway," Chrissy added, sadly. "He's tried to buy her from Derek Bute, but he won't sell her."

"Couldn't someone *tell* him?" Andrea said, indignantly.

"You can't tell that man *anything*," Chrissy replied. "Besides," she added, "it's difficult telling someone that sort of thing."

Andrea blushed. "Sue had a job telling me how badly I was riding Rags," she admitted.

"Oh Andy, don't worry," Chrissy put a hand on her shoulder. "You weren't anything like Derek Bute. You were a bit . . . unhappy, weren't you?" Andrea nodded. "Your riding is much better since the three-day event," Chrissy told her, reassuringly. "At least you listened to Sue."

"Is there anything we can do?" Adam asked, thinking of Cracker.

"I'm afraid not," Chrissy told him.

"Unless you beat Derek Bute tonight, Adam!" Tessa said, her eyes shining with her newly thought-up plan. "Then perhaps he'll give in and sell Cracker to Peter!"

"Have a heart!" Adam exclaimed. "I've hardly jumped Cindy yet!"

"Well, now's your chance!" Tessa told him excitedly.

"You're entering tonight, are you?" Chrissy asked Adam.

"Well . . ." Adam looked at the expectant faces round him, "it looks as though I am," he finished, with a grin.

The entrants began arriving soon after six, although the competition was not due to begin until seven thirty, with clear-round jumping at seven o'clock.

Cecil welcomed each new arrival with an excited bray, as he trotted alongside the cinder path. He had been allowed into the field for the day and had not yet been taken back to the orchard.

Several of the livery horses were entered. Their owners only needed to arrive in time to saddle up and warm up their horses in the exercise area outside. Some arrived straight from work, bringing their riding clothes with them. Derek Bute, who lived locally, arrived at ten to seven. His grey, sixteen hand mare, Cracker, was sweating from a hard ride over to the centre. Nervousness

61

quivered through her whole body, as she tried to interpret her rider's heavy-handed aids. Her ears were twitching backwards and forwards and she moved her head agitatedly.

Chrissy could not hide the dislike in her eyes, but her voice was noncommital as she spoke to Derek Bute. "You needn't have rushed," she told him, her hand resting on the mare's heavily sweating shoulder. "It's clear-round jumping first – you don't usually do that, do you?"

"Damn!" Derek Bute's face scowled as he wrenched the reins sideways, irritatedly. "I forgot that – it's just for the kids."

"I wouldn't say that —" Chrissy began, but Bute the Brute was gone, trotting his agitated mare out of the school.

"He'll be back – unfortunately," Chrissy muttered to Sandy.

The next ten minutes were busy for Andrea, who was taking the last-minute clear-round entries. Many of these were local youngsters with their ponies, although there were older riders too.

Sultan's big black head pushed against Chrissy's shoulder. Chrissy looked up at his rider. "Hello, Mrs Mountford," she said, "are you entering the competition?"

"Just the clear round," the older woman confessed. "I haven't plucked up courage to try the competition yet."

"Good for you! Better to take it slowly." Chrissy smiled up at her. Mrs Mountford was a bit of a fusspot, Chrissy decided, but she liked her, neverthless. Mrs Mountford adored her big-boned black gelding, which she kept at Heronsway. She rode him carefully, listening to her instructors. She had only recently taken up riding, and was a nervous but enthusiastic horsewoman.

"Are we ready, then?" Chrissy asked, her foot on the step leading up to the judges' box. "Sandy and Tessa – you're doing the jumps. And Kate, you're on the board and marshalling – OK? Sarah – you're general dogsbody between us all, and Andy's doing last-minute entries and the coffee bar." She grinned at Adam, who was mounted on Cindy, and looked somewhat apprehensive. "You're our sole representative, Adam," she told him. "Good luck!"

The clear-round jumping, with jumps of no more than one foot six, was always a popular event. The entry fee was low, and everyone who jumped a clear round received a rosette. Sandy and Tessa were kept busy in between rounds, replacing fallen bars or other parts of jumps, but at the end of the clear-round jumping a number of ponies sported rosettes. Towering above them was Sultan, his bridle fluttering with a rosette as Mrs Mountford patted his neck enthusiastically.

"Well done!" Chrissy called, as she climbed down from the judges' box to help with the jumps. There was no time to stop. The unaffiliated jumping competition was to follow straight on, as soon as the jumps had been raised.

The judge for the jumping competition arrived – a young woman called Meg, who lived locally and who would be judging at the horse show on Saturday.

"I'm not late, am I?" Meg asked, breathlessly, as she arrived at the top of the steps. "I had to get the kids to bed before I came out. What a rush!" she added.

"Perfect timing," said Chrissy. "We're just about to start." Ushering Meg into the box, and sending Sarah for a cup of coffee for her, Chrissy picked up the microphone of the loudspeaker system. "*Please* work," she muttered to it, as she pushed down the switch. Last week, Peter had been having some trouble with it, but now it seemed to be all right.

"Good evening, ladies and gentlemen." As her voice came over, loud and clear, Chrissy heaved a sigh of relief. Announcing the absence of Sue and Peter Venables, she introduced Meg as the judge for the evening and began the competition.

"First entry into the ring, please," she boomed over the system. Switching it off, she called out, urgently, "Sarah, quick! Where's the list? We don't know who's coming first!"

But as Sarah bounded up the steps with the list, Chrissy realized only too well who the first competitor was, as the gate opened and horse and rider entered the arena.

"Our first competitor this evening for the un-affiliated jumping competition," she said into the microphone, "is Mr Derek Bute riding Cracker."

9

Derek Bute thumped his legs against the grey's sides, sending her leaping into the school at a fast, disjointed canter.

"Calm down, you stupid beggar," he shouted at Cracker, pulling back his hands with a strength that made the watchers shudder as they saw the pelham bit jerk against the young mare's sensitive mouth. She threw her head up in alarm. The response from her rider was a sharp cut on the shoulder with his whip.

Hastily looking round to make sure that the jumps were in place, Chrissy pressed the bell, to inform Derek Bute that he could begin his round. As she circled before approaching the first jump, the grey mare pricked her ears. Forgetting her fear of her rider, Cracker tackled the course of jumps with evident pleasure. She managed to complete the course without penalties, despite her rider. He threw himself about in the saddle at every jump, shouted, cursed, and cut his mare across the flanks with his crop before each take-off.

"Clear round for Derek Bute on Cracker," Chrissy said, over the system. Switching off the microphone, she added, with disgust, "Thank goodness *that's* over."

"It's not a pretty sight," Meg agreed. "That poor creature. I wonder, sometimes, whether to use my position as judge to order Derek Bute off the course." She frowned. "But the trouble is he doesn't do anything downright cruel – and I know that he'd only have it out on her afterwards."

Chrissy confided Tessa's idea to Meg, but Meg shook her head. "He's a stubborn man," she said. "That type usually is. The more Peter tries to buy Cracker, the more determined Derek Bute will be to keep her."

The next competitor entered the ring. Chrissy announced her and pressed the bell. Meg was probably right about Derek Bute, she thought to herself, as she watched the girl set her bay pony at the first jump. They completed the course carefully, but knocked down the gate.

"Four faults," Chrissy called, over the loudspeaker system. "Pity about that," she commented, when she had switched off.

"Took off too early," said Meg. "Too flat a jump."

The competition continued. There were two more clear rounds. One was a young man who kept his liver chestnut gelding, Copper, at Heronsway. Copper was nearly sixteen hands high, half thoroughbred and half Arab. He was an attractive horse, strongly built, but with fine clean legs and a beautiful Arab head. He jumped boldly, and his rider rode him sensitively. Together, they cleared the jumps neatly and efficiently.

"I'll never beat *him*," Adam muttered disconsolately to Tessa, from Cindy's back.

"Don't be such a pessimist," Tessa hissed back

66

at him. She opened the door to let out the chestnut and his rider. "Number fourteen," she called, "into the ring, please!"

The other clear round came from a very solid-looking skewbald cob of about fifteen two, ridden by a woman in her forties who looked as if she had spent a lot of time in the saddle.

"They seem in tune with each other," Chrissy commented to Meg.

"Yes," the other agreed, "they're a good steady partnership. They usually do well – not so good on speed, though."

Then it was Adam's turn. His face was set and determined as he took Cindy through the gate into the indoor school. He and Cindy had jumped a couple of times – once over the practice jump outside and once over a small log during their ride to the Roman camp. But because of Sue's illness there had been little time for riding, let alone jumping.

"Come on, Cindy," Adam whispered, smoothing the bay mare's neck. "Let's show Bute the Brute!" He cantered her slowly round the arena.

When the bell rang, they headed for the first brush fence. This was quite low, and Cindy hopped over it easily. She took the next jump, parallel bars, in her stride, and continued easily round the course. As each jump was tackled, neatly and without mishap, Adam relaxed and began to enjoy himself. They jumped the last obstacle, the double, and passed the finish accompanied by a loud cheer from the Heronsway contingent.

Adam's grin was broad as he trotted his pony out of the school.

"That was great!" Sandy said, holding open the gate. "And no jumps to put back!"

Adam slid down from the saddle. He patted Cindy's neck. "I can't see why that Fiona girl treated her like she did," he said.

"She was another Bute the Brute," Tessa muttered, under her breath, since Derek Bute was nearby. "I bet Cracker would be as calm as Cindy is, with Peter riding her."

"I hope your plan works," Adam said. "But the next round will be timed — and Cracker and that lovely chestnut are fast —"

"Oh, Adam," Tessa broke in, impatiently, "Cindy's great. And you've got one advantage over the others."

"What's that?"

"She's smaller than them. That helps with an indoor course like this — Sue said so, when I was in the judges' box helping her, once."

Adam grinned. "I'll try, anyway," he said, cheerfully, leading Cindy away for a cool-down.

Five more competitors took part. One of them, Karen Stringer, a girl of about fifteen, rode her lovely palomino pony round the course without faults.

Chrissy announced a short break while the jumps were raised, and sent Sarah for two more cups of coffee. "It's thirsty work, this announcing," she told her with a grin.

Tessa and Sandy ran round the course of jumps, putting some up a notch or two, and removing some from the timed course by taking them down, putting a pole across slantwise and taking away the number. They put the correct numbers on the five jumps that had been left – the Road Closed, Wall, the Spread, Planks and the Double. They turned the double round to suit the new course, and raised the poles.

Chrissy inspected the new course and then returned to the judges' box. Meg had the jump-off sheet ready next to her cup of coffee, with the five competitors' names and numbers written in.

"Well," Meg said, her normally serious face breaking into a smile, "let battle commence! I don't have to guess which one you want to win – but the timer decides." She reached across with her left hand, closing her fingers round her stopwatch. "I'll use this one as a double check OK? If there's any doubt, we'll use my watch."

"Fine. Ready then?" Chrissy announced the order of the jump-off competitors, which had been given to her by Meg. Then she cast a quick look round the arena. She signalled to Kate, who opened the gate to allow the first competitor into the ring. It was the sturdy skewbald.

"First for the jump-off is Lesley Grower riding Patchwork," Chrissy announced, and she pressed the bell. Patchwork cantered steadily round in a wide circle, and then his rider set him towards the first jump, urging him on to a faster pace.

Meg and Chrissy leaned forward, watching closely through the wide glass window of the judges' box. As Patchwork passed the start line, both Meg's watch and the digital timer clicked, as the two starters were pressed.

The skewbald thundered round the course, his rider taking him steadily over each jump in turn. First the Road Closed and then the Wall. Sandy, watching from the gate at the side of the school, whispered to Tessa, "He's like a war-horse!"

"Well, this is going to be a battle, isn't it?" Tessa whispered back. They were both aware of Adam, watching tensely from Cindy's back, somewhere behind them in the shadows.

Inside the judges' box, Meg and Chrissy watched intently as Patchwork turned in a wide arc at the end of the indoor school and then cantered towards the Spread, which he jumped with ease, continuing across the arena to take the Planks in his stride. Another turn, and then he faced the Double. With two neat jumps he was past the finish, and the two timers clicked.

Chrissy and Meg conferred. "Clear round!" Chrissy announced, over the loudspeaker system, "with a time of 21.42 seconds."

Lesley Grower left the ring looking pleased and patting the skewbald, who snorted with pleasure. "That was a fast time for us," she told Tessa and Sandy.

Copper was called in next. Adam's fears seemed justified, since Copper and his young rider flew round the course, jumping without penalties and in a time of 20.97 seconds, which put them well into the lead.

"I can't see how I can beat that," Adam had moved out of the shadows to stand next to Sandy and Tessa at the gate.

"You don't really know yet what you and Cindy can do," Sandy pointed out. But now Adam was busy watching his main rival, Derek Bute.

As the big grey mare entered the ring, her rider gave her a couple of whacks across the shoulder.

70

"What was that for?" Adam muttered angrily.

"I expect he thinks if he gets her worked up she'll go faster," Tessa commented. And it must have seemed to Derek Bute that this theory worked, for Cracker cantered at a fast rate round the course, taking each jump easily and quickly, and turning fast at each end of the arena. The real reason for Cracker's speed, however, was that, for once, she was unimpeded by her rider's antics in the saddle. Derek Bute was not a good rider, and Cracker's enthusiasm sent her at such a speed that he had to concentrate on actually staying on! For once, Derek Bute had no time to shout or hit his horse, or throw himself about at each jump.

"A clear round," Chrissy announced, grudgingly, "with the time of 18.20 seconds." She gritted her teeth as she added, "With that fast time, Derek Bute and Cracker go into the lead."

A murmur ran around the indoor school as the time was announced. Adam was quiet as he watched the next competitor enter. It was Karen Stringer on her palomino pony, Sunshine. They were doing well, and were beating Derek Bute's time, when Sunshine just tipped the top bar of the spread. It clattered to the ground, and Karen's face reflected her disappointment.

"Four faults," Chrissy called into the microphone. "And now, our last competitor for the jump-off, Adam Maiyer, riding his pony, Cindy."

As Adam headed his pony towards the gate at the side of the jumping arena, he caught sight of Derek Bute. Lolling back in Cracker's saddle, he was watching Adam smugly, through narrowed eyes.

All at once, Adam knew that he and Cindy could do it. Leaning forward, as they cantered round prior to beginning the course, he spoke to Cindy, smoothing her brown neck. This was going to be it! The bell rang, and Adam turned his pony towards the start. He squeezed her on with his legs and his newly-found determination transmitted itself to Cindy. With ears pricked, she set herself at the first jump and flew over it. They surged over the Wall, and turned sharply into the Spread.

Sandy and Tessa, watching from the fence, held their breath. Adam had not left Cindy much room before this jump, but although Cindy was moving fast Adam had her under control, and they soared over the jump with inches to spare. Before the two girls had time to breathe a sigh of relief, Adam and Cindy were over the Planks and had turned hard again. This time they were faced with the Double. As they landed after the second jump, Adam leaned forward, giving Cindy a free rein, and the bay mare galloped flat out past the finish.

In the judges' box, Chrissy pressed the switch on the digital timer and peered at the time. She jumped up in excitement.

"17.93 seconds!" she squeaked excitedly to Meg. "Is that what you make it?"

Meg smiled. "That's right," she replied, "He's beaten Derek Bute. But," she added, quietly, "don't expect him to act according to your plan. I'm afraid you'll all be in for a disappointment."

But Chrissy was jubilant. Snatching up the microphone and switching it on, she announced, in a voice that could barely hide its delight,

"That time was the best this evening, ladies and gentlemen. 17.93 seconds for Adam Maiyer and Cindy, which makes them our winners. Well done, Adam." Then, remembering, she added, a little less enthusiastically, "Second is Derek Bute on Cracker." Her voice brightened as she continued, "Ian Coates is in third place on Copper, Lesley Grower is fourth, riding Patchwork and Karen Stringer takes fifth place with Sunshine."

As Chrissy accompanied Meg into the ring, holding the box which contained the rosettes and the first and second prizes, she looked towards the fence at the side of the indoor school. That face at the end, pale and drawn – surely it was . . . Yes! It was Peter!

10

"Is she better?"

"Is she all right?"

Dishevelled and weary, Peter smiled nonetheless. "Not exactly," he told them. "She's still unconscious – but there *is* an improvement. That's why I'm here."

"What —" Chrissy began, but Peter interrupted, as he continued. "I've been talking to her, you see," he said. "The doctors told me to do that. All the time. I've been telling her about the centre, and about how you're all helping." He stopped and looked round at them. "And today she started to say a few words," he finished.

"That's really marvellous," Chrissy said, "so why —"

"I'm here," Peter continued, anticipating her question, "because the doctor in charge of her case suggested that I make a tape of things happening here at Heronsway – and so I have!" He held up a small recording machine. "They lent me this at the hospital – they use it for recording letters for the secretaries – and I've taped some of the competition tonight. Chrissy's announcements, the sound of the horses' hooves, the jumps falling, ponies whinnying – everything. And now I'm going to take it back and play it to Sue. The doctor thinks it might help to bring her round.

He wants to get her properly conscious as soon as possible.

They didn't let him go straightaway. Sarah fetched Peter some coffee from the kitchen and Chrissy went to the caravan to fetch the clean clothes that he wanted. Meanwhile, Tessa and Sandy told him about their idea to get Derek Bute to sell Cracker.

"We didn't mean to bother you now, Peter," Sandy told him, "but we thought —"

Tessa took up the plea. "We thought that if you asked him now – well, he might be so fed up because Adam beat him that he might sell her this time."

"I'll have another try," Peter said, wearily. He was shaking his head as he spoke. "But I don't think it will work. I've already offered him more than I should. I'll try though."

It was no good. Meg and Peter had been right. Derek Bute was more determined than ever to keep his mare.

"I'll teach her a lesson," he told Peter. "She's not going to mess about when *I'm* riding her. She'll learn who's master – you'll see."

"But Derek." Giving up the idea of trying to persuade him to sell Cracker, Peter pleaded for the young mare. "She doesn't need mastery," he said, "she needs careful training. She's a highly-strung, sensitive horse. She's —"

But Derek Bute did not wait to hear what Peter thought. "She doesn't need your namby-pamby treatment," he broke in, "I know how to handle *her*." And he thrust his heels into the mare's sides, making her leap away in alarm.

Disappointment at the failure of Tessa's plan to persuade Bute the Brute to part with Cracker was lessened somewhat by Peter's instant agreement to the camping project.

"Seems a good idea to me," Peter agreed, drinking his coffee in the judges' box, after the competition was over. Adam had been delegated to ask, since it had been his idea in the first place. "You won't have to travel backwards and forwards all the time," Peter added.

"That's what we thought," said Adam.

"And as long as all the parents agree, of course," Peter added, putting down his mug and pushing back his chair. "Now, I must get back." He turned to Chrissy, who was packing up the judging sheets. "You're all doing a great job," he told her, quietly. "Let's hope I have some better news about Sue soon."

Cecil wasn't too sure about this invasion of his privacy. Since he had been let loose in the orchard, it had become *his* territory. The comings and goings were all very intriguing, of course, but these large white objects which were sprouting up in his orchard were taking up valuable eating space! However, the poles did make useful scratching posts.

"I vote we put Cecil in the field," Adam said,

as he watched his tent slide slowly to the ground for the third time, following Cecil's energetic scratching session against the pole.

"I think he probably needs delousing," Sandy admitted.

So Cecil was banished to the field and was liberally sprinkled with delousing powder by Sandy and Tessa.

"Right," said Adam, banging in the last tent peg, "I declare this campsite open! I'm hungry!" he added, looking hopefully towards the barbecue which Sarah had borrowed from her parents.

"This is to be a campsite of equal opportunity," Tessa told him, promptly. "Just because we females outnumber you, six to one, we still want to give you the opportunity to do the cooking! Here you are," she added, thrusting a bag of charcoal into his hands. "I'll fetch the food, then Sandy and I have to go and feed Mr Crichley's animals."

It had been a quietly busy day, and everyone was hungry by the time Adam called "Grub up!"

The building of the campsite had not begun until the evening, when most of the work at the centre had been completed. By the time everyone had arrived for Adam's meal, the warm summer evening was fading colourfully into night. The barbecue glowed welcomingly. Adam had put plates and mugs on the old trestle table that Chrissy had found behind the caravan.

Kate arrived with bottles of home-made apple juice and a huge bag of tomatoes. "Part of my wages from the fruit farm," she told them cheerfully.

Adam pointed to the trestle table. "It's self-service," he informed the others. "Jacket potatoes there. Bring your plates and I'll dish out the sausages and bacon. And there's a pan of baked beans under —" His hand reached down and came into contact with Freddie's head. "Oh no!" he wailed. Adam peered under the table. He stood up again, holding out the empty pan. "Freddie's eaten the beans," he announced.

"He'll eat *anything*, that animal," Chrissy sighed. "You're a bad, naughty boy!" she told him, but somehow the tone of voice didn't match the words. Freddie smiled up at her, his tongue still licking at the sides of his mouth, where tell-tale drops of baked-bean juice still lingered.

"I brought bread, too," Kate said, pulling out two long French sticks from her bag. "We'll have to fill up on that."

A contented silence settled on the campsite as the meal was quickly and appreciatively disposed of. No one took pity on Freddie, who watched the progress of all the food from plate to mouth, his head swinging from side to side like a spectator at a tennis match.

"You've had enough, Freddie," Chrissy said, firmly. Freddie hiccoughed reproachfully.

"You ate two big tins of baked beans!" Adam told him.

"He'll be sick," Tessa yawned as she spoke, leaning back against a bale of straw. Chrissy had dragged the bales from where they had been stacked, next to the henhouse. They were comfortable to lean against. "Great meal, Adam," Tessa added, sleepily, "I might even wash up."

"I'll help," Sandy said. She, too, suddenly felt tired.

"This was a good idea, Adam," she added. "I really feel as if I'm on holiday, now."

"I've never been camping before," Andrea observed.

"As long as you don't snore," said Sarah, who was sharing a tent with her. Andrea retorted by tipping Sarah sideways, which in turn knocked Sandy against Freddie, who leapt up, thinking that this was a new game that he wasn't going to be left out of. The trestle table went flying and with it the dirty plates. A state of hilarity then took over the Heronsway campsite, continuing throughout the washing up, a communal affair which took place in the cramped conditions of the caravan.

At last, worn out with the work of the day and the laughter of the evening, they made for their various tents. As a concession to normal home behaviour, they all cleaned their teeth in the caravan, and then, with sleepy goodnights, retired to bed.

"Let's say goodnight to Cecil, first," Sandy suggested to Tessa. Cecil, still in exile in the field, stood by the orchard gate, watching the campers forlornly.

"Poor little Cecil," Sandy put her arm round his neck, which was beginning to feel a lot less scraggy already. "You want to come in, too, don't you?"

"You'll be back in your orchard on Saturday," Tessa told him, rubbing his grey neck. She yawned. "I can't stay up any longer," she stated. "Goodnight, Cecil – sleep well!"

Chrissy and Kate had retired to the caravan with Freddie. Sarah and Andrea were talking inside their tent, which glowed eerily from the light of a torch. Their low murmurs floated out into the late evening air of the orchard. Adam's tent, pitched under one of the old apple trees, was silent.

Tessa switched on her torch and opened her zip-up bag. "Mum made me put in pyjamas," she told Sandy, "but I don't think I can be bothered."

Sandy yawned, loudly. "I think I'll just take off my jeans," she agreed, sitting down on her sleeping bag to begin.

In two minutes, the girls were in their sleeping bags and were drifting off to sleep. The campsite was quiet, the silence broken only by the cry of a screech owl, far off, somewhere across the moors.

It felt like only a few minutes, but it must have been at least two hours later when Sandy awoke. She lay in her sleeping bag, staring at the sloping canvas roof of the tent, trying to think where she was. She remembered, as the noise came. She sat up. That must have been what had woken her. It was a sound which she couldn't quite pin down, followed by a grunting noise which she knew only too well.

Cecil rarely brayed, but he often made a peculiar little grunting, snorting sound, usually when he didn't want to do something, like move away from a particularly luscious area of grass.

Sandy leaned back on her elbows. A wave of tiredness swept over her. Should she bother to investigate? Cecil was probably just annoyed at not being able to get into the orchard. Then Sandy contemplated the possibility that he had tried to get in, and was stuck somehow. The thought of Cecil caught on barbed wire got her out of her sleeping bag and into her jeans. Slipping on her shoes, Sandy pushed open the flap of the tent and poked her head through the opening.

It was well and truly night now. A delicate crescent moon was flying in a cloudless night sky, against which trees and hedges were etched, black and intricately formed.

Sandy breathed in the heavy scent of a summer night. Her eyes accustoming themselves to the dark, she looked towards the field. She was too low down to see anything except the hedge. Standing up, Sandy strained her eyes to find Cecil. Then the noise came again, from somewhere to her right. She swung round. There he was!

Cecil wasn't stuck. He seemed to be standing, feet planted firmly, in the field. But Cecil wasn't alone. A dark shape was beside him. It seemed to be a man, who was tugging at a halter which was round Cecil's head.

Someone was trying to steal Cecil!

11

"Tess! Wake up!"

A grunt was the only response to Sandy's urgent whisper, so she shook the unresponsive contents of Tess's sleeping bag. "Come on, Tess. Wake up, *please*!"

At last Tessa's tousled fair hair emerged from the sleeping bag, followed by a pair of puzzled grey eyes, blinking with tiredness. Pushing herself up on one elbow, Tessa rubbed at her eyes with her other hand and yawned.

"Sandy," she complained, "it's the middle of the night and I was asleep. Don't you think —"

But Sandy cut her short. "I know all that," she whispered, impatiently, "but this is urgent. Someone's in the field, trying to steal Cecil!"

Tessa blinked at her. "Are you sure you're not just being imaginative?" she began. "You know what you're like —"

"Oh, Tess," Sandy tugged at her friend in exasperation. "Stop grumbling and come on. We've got to *do* something. There's a man out there and he's taking Cecil. And we've got to stop him," she continued, unzipping Tessa's sleeping bag and handing her her jeans. "*Now*," she added, in a determined tone.

Seeing that her friend really meant business, Tessa quickly pulled on her jeans. "Where'my-shoes?" she muttered incoherently, fumbling about at the end of her sleeping bag. "Can't see anything. Where's the torch?"

"No!" Sandy hissed, pushing the shoes towards her. "Don't put it on. He'll see."

Tessa, wide awake now, and dressed, stared at her friend from her sitting position. "You really mean it, don't you?" she whispered.

"'Course I do. Come on!"

"No. Wait a minute." Tessa rubbed her nose, thoughtfully, in the gloom of the tent. "We can't cope on our own. He might be armed."

"Armed!"

"Well, you know," Tessa replied, vaguely, "stick, or a cudgel, or something."

Sandy grinned, despite her fast-beating heart. "And he'll be wearing one of those masks with holes for his eyes!" she giggled. Still, she knew what Tessa meant.

"Anyway," Tessa said, stubbornly, still sitting on the ground, "I don't think we ought to tackle him alone. Let's wake Adam."

"Mm. OK." Sandy conceded, "but we'll have to hurry," she added. "He might have persuaded Cecil to move by now." Quickly she explained about Cecil's stubborn stance in the field. "I think the man was probably getting annoyed," Sandy added.

They planned their strategy in low whispers, and then stealthily crept from the tent. Adam's tent was only a few yards away. As they crawled carefully and quietly between the two tents, they could hear grunting and heavy breathing coming from the other side of the hedge, accompanied by what sounded like muffled swearing.

Working according to their plan, the two girls opened the flap of Adam's tent. They could just see a recumbent lump. Stealthily, they crept up on Adam. His sleeping face was turned towards Tessa's side, so she was the one who clamped a hand firmly over his mouth as she shook him awake. Adam's eyes shot open, and stared at them incredulously as stifled words were uttered indignantly behind Tessa's hand.

"It's all right, Adam," Sandy whispered. "It's only us – Tessa and Sandy. Don't talk out loud. Just whisper." Tessa released her hold.

"Whatever —" Adam began, but Tessa's hand flew to his mouth again for a moment.

"Shh. Be *quiet*, Adam," she whispered, impatiently, "there's someone out there."

Whispering quickly and urgently, they told him about the man. "And we're going to rescue Cecil," Tessa said, "with your help. Are you dressed?"

Adam sat up, blinking sleepily. "Yes," he whispered back, "I was too tired to bother with undressing last night." He pulled himself out of the sleeping bag and crouched, with the other two, in the shadowy light of the tent. "What are you going to do?" he asked.

"Just go and stop him – now we've got you," Sandy said. She turned towards the tent flap. "We'd better hurry," she added.

On the way, Adam picked up his torch, which was a large, heavy one, borrowed from his father. "I could hit him over the head with it, if necessary," he whispered to the other two, who nodded approvingly. They were feeling a little better about the proposed confrontation with the donkey thief, now that Adam had swelled their numbers. Even so, Sandy felt herself trembling as they crawled, on all fours, towards the orchard gate, and Tessa's stomach was turning over, uncomfortably. Adam never did own up to the two girls how much his heart was pounding.

The orchard gate was only a light one. Silently lifting the latch, Adam pushed it open. It squeaked slightly as they crawled through, one at a time. Tessa had a sudden urge to laugh as she crawled through the long grass on her hands and knees. She buried her head in the grass to stifle her giggles. Sandy prodded her from behind and they continued.

Adam, who was leading, came to a halt. Nearly bumping into him, Tessa looked up. Her heart lurched. They were right behind the man, who had stopped to blow breath.

"Come on, Donk, come on, there's a good boy." The hoarse whisper was wheedling. However, Cecil stood his ground, his ears flopped sideways and his neck stuck out, obstinately. The man's tone soon changed.

"Come *on*," he growled, jerking with all his strength on the rope. "Come on, you stupid —"

"Stop that!" Adam had sprung up from the grass. He pushed the end of the torch into the small of the man's back. "Don't move!" Adam commanded dramatically.

Tessa jumped up, too. Reaching over to Cecil's shaggy grey head, she snatched the halter and pulled it off, leaving it dangling from the man's hand.

Sandy, who had leapt up on the other side,

85

confronted the man. "What do you think you're doing?" she demanded, "stealing our —" She stopped, staring at the man incredulously. "Mr Bute!" she exclaimed. "Whatever are you doing here? Why would *you* want to steal Cecil?"

Derek Bute turned on the three of them angrily.

"He's mine!" he snarled at them, snatching Adam's torch from his hand. "I'm just taking back what belongs to me. I saw him in the field when I came to the jumping competition," he added. He glared at them. "You must have stolen him from me," he growled, adding, under his breath, "interfering kids." He waved the torch at them menacingly. "Well, now I'm taking him back!"

12

"Oh no, you're not, Mr Bute!"

They all swung round. It was Chrissy who had spoken. She and Kate were standing just behind them, in the long grass. Between the two of them stood Freddie, looking reassuringly large and un-puppyish in the moonlight. His hackles were raised and he gave a low growl. Derek Bute didn't look quite so sure of himself.

"Now look here," he began. His voice had its wheedling tone again.

"No, *you* look here, Mr Bute." Chrissy stepped forward a pace, tightening her grip on Freddie's lead. She was glad that she had decided to put his lead on him. Otherwise, he might have been gambolling in the grass, acting the fool as he so often did. He would stop and rest his front legs along the ground, leaving his bottom up in the air, while his long shaggy tail waved excitedly, and his eyes danced mischievously as he barked to them to come and play. Not the kind of position from which to confront a thief at midnight!

"But, but ..." Derek Bute spluttered. Patience was a rare part of Derek Bute's character, and it seemed to have been used up already. "This is *my* donkey!" he roared, waving towards Cecil. How-ever, Cecil had grown tired of this early morning meeting and had wandered away into the darkness.

When they all looked in the direction of Derek Bute's waving hand, nothing was to be seen but the grass, shining in the moonlight.

Annoyed, Derek Bute turned back. "He's *my* donkey," he repeated angrily, "and I want him back. You stole him from me!"

"Then why didn't you report the theft to the police?" Adam seemed to have grown at least two inches as he stood, glaring at Derek Bute, his chin jutting forward stubbornly. "We all know why," Adam continued, his voice hard with anger. "You were breaking the law by tethering that donkey so cruelly. The person who took him – and it wasn't us – was rescuing him from cruel treatment. The police know that – and they will be glad to know that we've found the donkey's owner, Mr Bute!"

There was a long silence. Derek Bute was beaten and he knew it, but he kept trying. "Come on, now," he wheedled, breaking the silence at last. "I love my little Donk. I just want to take him home and look after him."

"Huh! We know what you're like with animals," Tessa said.

"I tell you what, Mr Bute." It was Chrissy's voice, calm and quiet, which broke in. "I have a proposition to make."

Derek Bute looked at her in surprise, and so did the others. Surely Chrissy didn't want to begin any bargaining with Derek Bute?

But Chrissy looked confident, and there was a hint of a smile at the corners of her mouth as she continued. "We won't give you back your donkey. But we won't tell the police that it was you who owned him – if *you* will sell Cracker to

Peter Venables." She paused, and then added, "at Peter's price, of course!"

"You were fantastic, Chrissy!" Sandy, her feet tucked under her on the caravan seat, leaned forward and helped herself to another piece of toast. Everyone had declared themselves to be starving when they had seen Derek Bute off the premises, and had congregated at the caravan. Chrissy and Kate had made hot buttered toast and cocoa, while Sandy and Tessa had gone to wake up Andrea and Sarah, who had slept through it all.

"Unbelievable," Tessa agreed, mumbling through a mouthful of toast. "I'd never have thought of that."

"It was brilliant!" Adam stated.

"*Why* didn't you wake us?" wailed Sarah. "We've missed everything!"

"There wasn't time," Sandy explained. "We thought he might actually *steal* Cecil if we waited. We just woke Adam and went."

"But you two were there." Andrea turned to Chrissy and Kate. Chrissy grinned. "That was only because of Freddie," she explained. Freddie, sitting bolt upright between Chrissy and Kate, was enjoying his favourable reception – particularly when it was accompanied by toast! "Better not give him too much," Chrissy said, "I don't want him being sick again. That's how Kate and I arrived on the scene," she told them. "Freddie was feeling decidedly ill, after the baked beans episode, so I decided to take him outside. Then I could see

89

something was going on in the field, so I came back and fetched Kate, too!"

"Good old Freddie!" Adam ruffled Freddie's ears. "You looked quite fierce!"

Andrea leant down and put her arms round Freddie's neck. "You've helped to rescue Cecil *and* Cracker," she told him. "You're a very clever boy." She looked up at Chrissy. "Derek Bute really *did* promise, did he?" she asked.

"He did," Chrissy replied, "and if he goes back on it, he'll be in trouble, won't he? But . . ." She looked round at them all. "Perhaps we shouldn't tell our parents about all this. It does seem a bit like bribery, doesn't it?" There was a murmur of agreement from the Heronsway campers.

"I shall feel happier when Cracker actually belongs to Peter," Sandy admitted. She thought about her letter to Aunt Cress. "And when we find somewhere permanent for Cecil," she added.

Right on cue, Cecil's long grey mournful face appeared in the doorway of the caravan. A unanimous decision had allowed him back into the orchard. Now he was sure that something exciting was happening, and he felt that he was being left out.

Chrissy leaned forward and offered Cecil a piece of toast, which he crunched up happily.

"And now," Chrissy said, yawning loudly, "I really think that the Heronsway rescue team should all go back to bed. We've got to be up to see to the horses in three hours' time!"

In the morning it all seemed slightly unreal, but

Cecil, grazing contentedly back in his orchard instead of in the field, was a visible sign that *something*, at least, had happened. Freddie's somewhat woebegone expression and the campers' own reluctance to get up reminded them that the adventure with Derek Bute had, indeed, taken place.

Breakfast, eaten in and around the caravan, consisted of cereal, with milk which Chrissy had fetched earlier from the farm next door.

"Back to normal, now," Chrissy said, pouring from the jug of fresh, slightly warm milk.

Tessa poured some into her bowl too. "Hardly normal!" she pointed out. "Heronsway with no owners around, and a big gymkhana tomorrow!"

"And," Sandy reminded her, "old Mr Crichley comes home today."

"Mm." Tessa spoke between mouthfuls of cornflakes and milk. "but we can't hang about for too long waiting for him, can we? There's such a lot to do here. Hey, Chrissy," she added, "this milk's gorgeous! I thought I didn't like milk much."

"That's because it's fresh," Chrissy told her, "straight from the cow!"

"We could leave him a note," Sandy suggested, her mind still concerned with old Mr Crichley, "and a box of chocolates or something – Mum'll let me have one cheap, I expect. We must welcome him back. Mrs Loxton said he hadn't any family."

"Just his animals!" Tessa said. "OK, Florence Nightingale, note and chocs it is."

But old Mr Crichley arrived before the girls had finished feeding his animals. He had somehow persuaded the ambulance driver to drop him off first, even though it was out of his way, and he arrived just as the two girls had finished cleaning out the hutches. Earlier, they had been sent down to the shops by Mrs Loxton to buy provisions for the old man's store-cupboard, and so they were later than usual.

Accompanied by Monty, Tessa was busy pushing hay into the sleeping quarters, while Sandy filled the food bowls and checked the drinking bottles. Monty bounded down the path when he saw the old man opening the gate. They greeted each other delightedly, and old Arthur Crichley shuffled up the path, accompanied by his excited dog.

"Hello, Mr Crichley," Tessa said, closing the door of the end hutch. "Your animals are fine. They're all fed and cleaned out and Monty has had his walk."

The old man turned his penetrating blue eyes onto the two girls. "You've been champion, have you two girls," he told them. Then he noticed the open shed door. "What about my poor little Cecil?" he asked, anxiously, "He's not . . . he's not —"

"Oh no, Mr Crichley," Tessa answered, hastily, remembering Cecil that morning, very much alive as he had poked his head in through the caravan door. "Cecil's fine. He's in an orchard for now, and he's looking much better."

"And we've got lots to tell you," said Sandy. "We found his owner – or rather his owner found us."

The old man's eyes glinted angrily. "That's someone I'd like to meet!" he growled. "I'd give him a piece of my mind, and no mistake!"

"We'll tell you all about it," Sandy promised, "but first, Mrs Loxton wants to make you a cup of tea."

13

"Chrissy! The course builder has arrived!" Sandy, standing by the sliding door at the entrance to the indoor school, called in.

"Chrissy!" Andrea was calling, too, but from the other end of the school. She was leaning round the office door with the telephone receiver in one hand. "Launders on the phone. They say the rosettes are only just ready and they're sorry but they've missed the delivery van. Could someone collect them from Thelham?"

Chrissy stood in the middle of the indoor school, watching while a pupil rode Poppy, one of the Heronsway ponies, round the arena at a collected canter.

She turned away to call back to Sandy, "Take him to the jumping field, can you? I'll be there shortly."

"Good, Mary. That's much better," she told Poppy's rider. Then to Andrea she called, "I expect so – find out where and when!"

A general feeling of excitement was running through Heronsway. The adventure of last night, together with the preparations for the gymkhana tomorrow, had been added to by a telephone call from Peter. He had phoned to say that there had been a slight improvement in Sue's condition. There hadn't been time to talk about it much, since everyone was so busy, but the excitement was there.

During the afternoon, the centre's cross-country course had to be taken down, and the jumps stacked away. Then, Brian Golder, the course builder, arrived in a huge lorry to erect the course of jumps for the jumping events. Soon, a magnificent course stood in one field. A caravan was already in place to house the judges for the jumping competitions, and in the next field, Sandy, Tessa and Adam had erected a small marquee for the judges of the showing competitions.

In the third field, which was nearest to the office, Andrea and Sarah were arranging the poles for the bending race, and storing the sacks, buckets and other necessities for the gymkhana events in a small tent. Andrea was kept busy running to answer the telephone, which summoned her by means of an outside bell.

"I'm going to be so fit, I'll win the Walk, Trot and Lead easily," she exclaimed breathlessly, arriving back from a call. She had brought a jug of orange squash and glasses from the kitchen. Everyone gathered by the marquee thankfully and took a break.

"I don't suppose we'll be able to take part in anything," Tessa pointed out. "We'll be too busy!"

They all agreed afterwards that it had been a great day. There *had* been some problems, of course, but Sue's general organization had proved excellent. The show had been well-publicized beforehand, and by eight thirty in the morning horseboxes began trundling in. Competitors arrived on horse-back and spectators came in cars and on foot. The weather was still perfect. Soon there were horses, ponies and people milling everywhere.

Miraculously, the loudspeaker system played no unkind tricks, and Chrissy's voice came over loud and clear.

"Good morning, ladies and gentlemen. Can we have entrants for Class number one, Best Turned-out Horse and Rider, in the collecting ring of Ring One, please." She paused, and then continued, "And in Ring Three, please will entrants for Clear-Round jumping make their way to *that* collecting ring. Thank you!"

Chrissy turned off the microphone.

"That's it," she said to Adam, who was standing by with all the announcement details. "We've begun. Let's hope nothing goes wrong!"

Nothing did go wrong – until later on in the morning. And then the problem turned out to be more in the nature of an entertainment for the spectators!

Sarah had been allocated the job of steward to attend the judges and to carry messages between the rings. Late in the morning, she arrived, breath-lessly, at the collecting ring for Ring One, where Sandy and Mr Maiyer were busy taking numbers of competitors for Class number four, Best Working Hunter, fourteen hands and under.

"Sandy, there's someone at the gate asking for you," Sarah explained.

"I can't come. Who is it?"

"I think it's your old man. The one with the donkey. He says he's come to see Cecil."

"You go," said Mr Maiyer, leaning over and taking Sandy's notes from her. "I can manage. We've got most of them now."

So Sandy made her way to the gate, where old Mr Crichley waited.

"Sorry, Mr Crichley, I can't stay long," she said, "but I can show you where he is."

She took the old man over to the orchard, where Cecil was watching the proceedings with interest. Old Mr Crichley was delighted with the change in his stolen donkey.

"I'm sorry I can't stay," Sandy repeated, "I'll be by Ring One." Closing the gate, she hurried away, leaving them both in the orchard.

It was later on, as the ponies and horses for the next hunter class paraded round the ring, that a titter ran through the ranks of spectators.

"What's the matter?" Chrissy whispered to Adam, her hand over the microphone. Adam leaned over, peering round the ample forms of Mrs Cronin and Colonel Cox, the judges for this event. Then, grinning widely, Adam sat back in his chair. "You'll be able to see in about two seconds!" he told Chrissy, "when he comes into sight!"

"Adam! Don't be so mysterious! What —"

But Chrissy did not need to question Adam further. At that moment, the reason for the spectators' laughter became apparent. As the last of the hunters walked sedately past the judges' box, its neatly trimmed tail held proudly, a far less well-turned out competitor followed. It was a gate-crasher with long grey ears and an eager expression on his elongated face. Cecil gazed round him with a benign expression, and then hurried after the chestnut horse, somewhat similar in colour and build to Quest.

It had to be admitted that Cecil was not a pretty sight. Tessa and Sandy had concentrated on getting Cecil back to health, rather than bothering with grooming. They had treated him successfully for lice, but had not attempted, as yet, to deal with his matted grey coat. On his neck, where his tethering rope had rubbed him sore, Sandy had cut away the grey hair and had treated the sore area with pink antiseptic lotion, but everywhere else the long matted coat hung down, untidily. Cecil was much fitter – but he was a mess!

"Oh no!" Chrissy's voice wailed over the loud-speaker system and the spectators then felt free to laugh openly. Someone ducked underneath the rope fence and tried to lure Cecil out of the ring, but he trotted away, indignantly. He wasn't going to miss this fun!

"Sandy!" Chrissy decided to make use of the loudspeaker system to call for help. "Or Tessa! Can you come to Ring One, please, and remove Cecil!"

Back at her post, Sandy turned and was horrified to see where Cecil had appeared. Old Mr Crichley must have left the gate unfastened! Grabbing a convenient piece of rope, she ran towards the errant donkey.

"Cecil! Come on, there's a good boy." Cecil seemed pleased to see her and allowed the rope to be slipped round his neck. But leaving the ring was another matter. Quite definitely no, said Cecil! The more Sandy pulled, the more Cecil resisted and the more the spectators laughed! The hunters began to trot round the ring, while Sandy and Cecil continued their battle.

Much to Sandy's relief, Tessa arrived. "Go and fetch Quest," she suggested. "Cecil's sure to come then."

Sandy was only too pleased to leave the battle ground. While Tessa and Cecil stood in the ring, Sandy ran to Quest's stable, where the chestnut mare was waiting.

The younger Heronsway helpers had all groomed their ponies in readiness for the show. However, they had decided that the only possible time for any of them to compete would be during the afternoon, in the gymkhana games. So, eagerly watching the show from their stables were Quest, Duskie, Rags, Puffin and Cindy.

The chestnut pony whinnied a greeting as Sandy hurried past the row of stables towards her. Inside the stable, Sandy couldn't resist a quick hug, despite the urgency of her mission. She rubbed the beautiful mare's shining neck.

"You're coming to persuade your friend Cecil to stop parading round the ring and go back to his orchard," Sandy told her, as she slipped the bridle over Quest's head. "He thinks he's a fourteen hand hunter!" she added, fastening the buckle on the throat lash.

Quest, bored with waiting in her stable while horses and ponies trotted past the entrance to the stable yard, pranced and jogged on the spot when Sandy let her out. She snorted and tossed her head. Sandy jumped up onto her bare back.

"Now, into the showring with you, Questie," she murmured, "to de-donkey the hunter class!"

Cecil became meek and pliable as soon as Quest arrived. Amid cheers and clapping from the spectators, Sandy and Quest jogged out of the showring, followed by a demure, shabby little donkey. Cecil was soon back in his orchard, and the gate was firmly latched. Reluctantly, Sandy put Quest back in her stable, promising her a ride later on.

The morning continued, and the showing classes finished. In Ring Three, the Clear-Round jumping was drawing to a close.

Inwardly breathing a sigh of relief, Chrissy announced a brief lunch break before the gymkhana games, and had the judges' lunches brought to the marquee.

Andrea didn't win the Walk, Trot and Lead race, but she and Rags finished third in their event. Tessa and Duskie came second in their heat in the Bending race, but were knocked out in the final, in which Sarah and Puffin came third. Sandy and Quest were second in the Musical Sacks event, but Adam and Cindy were unsuccessful in the Chase-me-Charlie.

By the time the gymkhana events had finished and horseboxes followed each other down the cinder track to the lane, everyone was feeling tired but cheerful.

"I could sleep for a week!" Adam said, yawning. They had congregated in a small group by the marquee. Chrissy, who had just said goodbye to the last of the judges, looked at him with a grin.

"You aren't allowed to be tired yet," she told

him, briskly. "We've got all the clearing up of litter to do yet!"

They all groaned, but everyone was too weary to argue. Chrissy handed out black plastic bags, and the five younger members, plus Kate, set out in different directions to begin the clearing-up process. Bottles, cartons and paper bags were retrieved from the grass and under hedges, and the plastic bags began to fill up.

Intent on their work, the helpers did not notice a shabby little car bump its way down the cinder path towards the equestrian centre. Freddie noticed, however, and he went bounding off in the direction of the office.

"Hello, everyone!" It was Chrissy's voice, floating out over the foot and hoof-trodden grass of the empty fields. Over the loudspeaker system, Chrissy's voice sounded high-pitched, almost squeaky with excitement. "Drop everything!" it ordered, dramatically, "and come to the marquee. We've got some wonderful news!"

14

Peter Venables was in the marquee with Chrissy. His face was tired and drawn, but he was smiling broadly.

"You did it!" he told them happily. "The tape, with all of you on it – it did the trick!"

"Is Sue better, then?" Tessa asked, excitedly.

"Yes." Peter's voice was as thrilled as Tessa's. "She's fully conscious. Very tired, of course, but she's her old self." Peter looked round at them all. "She sent the message that she's very, *very* grateful to you all for keeping the centre going."

"It was Chrissy, really," Sandy pointed out.

"But I couldn't have managed without you all," Chrissy protested.

"Well, anyway," Peter continued, "we're both very grateful to you *all*. Sue and I have agreed that I should come back to look after things now that she's off the danger list."

"But she's surely not better yet – from the meningitis, I mean?" Chrissy asked.

Peter shook his head. "It wasn't meningitis, after all," he told her. "All the symptoms were right – stiff neck, very bad headache, tiredness – but the tests proved negative. They don't know what she has had," he added, "it seemed to be a mystery virus. The main thing is – she's better!"

They celebrated with coffee and cheese sandwiches in the coffee bar.

"It's all that's left," Chrissy explained, digging into a box in search of packets of crisps.

"They're the best sandwiches I've ever tasted," said Peter. "I don't seem to have eaten properly for a week." He pulled an envelope from his top pocket. "By the way," he said, slowly, "can anyone tell me anything about this?" He withdrew a sheet of paper from the envelope and stared at it, a puzzled expression on his face. "It's from Derek Bute, of all people." Peter looked up. "I just can't understand it," he said. "Derek wants me to telephone him. Says he's willing to sell Cracker, after all." Peter looked round at the Heronsway helpers. "Whatever can have made him change his mind?" he asked them.

Sandy and Tessa looked at each other and then at Adam. They hadn't discussed the possibility of telling Peter about their midnight meeting with Derek Bute. Suddenly, the whole agreement with Bute the Brute seemed a little on the shady side. They looked back towards Chrissy, who opened her mouth to speak.

"Have another sandwich!" Kate pushed the plate under Peter's nose, and at the same time the telephone rang. Thankfully, Chrissy escaped to the office. The guilty secret was still theirs!

As they cycled slowly home in the evening, the camp having broken up, Sandy and Tessa discussed it.

"I must admit I feel badly about it," Sandy told her friend.

"I can't see why," Tessa replied.

Freewheeling down the incline from the motorway bridge, Sandy tried to explain. "Well, we *are* sort of bribing him, aren't we?"

"Derek Bute, do you mean? Well, he deserves it!"

"But it was *his* donkey, even though he didn't look after it. And we are kind of stealing Cecil by not giving him back."

"Mmm."

"P'raps I'll go and see him tomorrow." Sandy, having made her decision, looked to her friend for approval.

"I can't see what good that'll do," Tessa argued, "but if you really want to," she added, with a sigh, knowing Sandy's determination in these matters, "I suppose I'll come with you."

"Thanks."

It was Tessa's turn to look across from her bike. "But what will you do – offer to *buy* Cecil?"

Sandy frowned. "I suppose I'll have to," she admitted. "I've got a bit of money saved up for a pony. I didn't really want to buy a donkey, but . . ."

The rest of Sandy's sentence was left to drift as unspoken thoughts in the warm evening air of the narrow country lane, as the two bicycles turned right towards Clereton town centre.

Derek Bute's cottage was on the other side of the road which led into Clereton. Beyond a narrow bridge which went over the disused railway line, a stony, rutted track led to the small cottage. Once it had been whitewashed, but now the outside was a dirty grey. A small lawn at the front of the cottage had been recently mown and two tubs by the front door were filled with geraniums, but the rest of the property looked shabby.

As the two girls pushed their bicycles down the track, they could see Derek Bute in his yard. He was bending down beside a somewhat dilapidated-looking motorbike which rested against the wall of an old stable. Next to the stable was a lean-to shed which contained logs, a few bales of hay and some old tarpaulins. The stable and shed were attached to the cottage. On the third side of the yard a five-bar gate led into the smallest orchard the girls had ever seen. A little girl played near the gate, and watching them from the orchard was Cracker.

The tiny orchard had obviously been a quagmire earlier in the year, when there had been a lot of rain. Now, the ground was baked hard, with barely any sign of grass.

"I hope he hasn't changed his mind," Tessa whispered to Sandy, as they approached slowly. "I can't see how Cracker can survive in that little place, with no grass."

"Perhaps he gives her hay," Sandy suggested. "There's some in the shed." She cleared her throat, noisily. "Er . . . hello, Mr Bute," she said.

Derek Bute swung round. At first, Sandy thought he looked angry. Then she could see that his eyes were defensive.

"What d'you want?" he asked, tersely.

"It's . . . it's about the donkey," Sandy began, hesitantly.

"Now, look here!" Derek Bute's face reddened. "We had all that out, Thursday night. You said —"

"We said that we wouldn't give you back your donkey," Tessa broke in.

104

"And that doesn't seem very fair," Sandy contributed.

"Now you look here," Derek Bute repeated, angrily, his temper getting the better of him as usual, "I don't *want* him back!"

Sandy and Tessa looked at each other and then back at Derek Bute.

"I've never been on the wrong side o' the law," Derek Bute explained, his voice quieter as he calmed down, "and I don't want to be now. I don't want that donkey, neither," he continued, "it's been more trouble than it's worth. I only got him for my little Angie there." He jerked his head in the direction of the little girl.

Derek Bute continued to tell the girls of how he had swopped his old car – which he had been going to take to the scrapyard, anyway – for the donkey. He had thought that the donkey would make a good pet for his little girl, but Angie had soon lost interest. Then Derek Bute, too, had grown tired of looking after the donkey. He had no grazing, and was having to feed hay to Cracker, so he had tethered the donkey some way from home. He admitted to Sandy and Tessa that he had not looked after it properly.

"I was busy, and my wife was ill and . . . I sort of forgot about him," he told them. "Then, when I went to see him and he was gone – well, I thought the police had found him. I was real worried, I can tell you." Derek Bute rested a hand on the saddle of his motorbike. "I'd heard about that new law, too, you see," he continued. "Then, when I saw him there in the equestrian centre – well, I thought I'd get him back and be in the clear!" He shook his head, sadly, "I just want to be rid of him," he told the girls. "He didn't cost me anything – but he'd cost me something if I landed up in court, and no mistake!"

A huge expression of relief spread over Sandy's face. "Well, that's all right then, Mr Bute," she told him. Derek Bute looked at her doubtfully, and Sandy continued. "Because I know where your donkey can have a home and be looked after – for the rest of his life!"

15

"Why didn't you tell me?" Tessa, pushing hard against the pedals as she rode her bicycle up the slope of the railway bridge, called out over her shoulder.

"I tried to," Sandy replied, following in Tessa's wake, "but you started asking me what Aunt Cress's name was short for, and then we got on to the soap at Christmas. We never got round to what she was writing about in her letter!"

"Derek Bute seemed really pleased, didn't he?"

"He doesn't seem so bad after all, does he?" Sandy brought her bike alongside Tessa's when they reached the wider part of the road. "He just seems to have such a quick temper. I don't think he means to be cruel. It's like P. C. Thrower said about people just being thoughtless. He'll be better with motorcycle racing," she concluded, "he seemed to be quite keen about that!"

Tessa giggled. "Peter was surprised to see us, wasn't he, when he came to fetch Cracker?" she said.

"I think we're going to have to own up to Peter," Sandy said.

Sandy was right. As soon as Peter had bedded Cracker down in her new stable, leaving her plenty of hay, he searched out the two girls. They were in the tack room, where Sarah was washing off Puffin's bit and Andrea was rubbing up her saddle. Chrissy and Adam came in with more tack over their arms, and Sandy was just about to tell them the good news when Peter arrived.

"Now come on, you two," he began, "what have you been up to? I thought it was strange that Derek had changed his mind. Then, when I saw you both at his cottage —"

"It wasn't them, Peter," Chrissy broke in, "it was me. I . . ." She paused and took a deep breath before continuing, "I'm afraid I sort of *bribed* Derek Bute!"

"No, you didn't, Chrissy," Tessa told her quickly, "because he didn't want —"

"Now, come on!" It was Peter's turn to interrupt. He sat down on a bale of hay and looked round at them all with a mixture of amusement and concern on his face. "I think you'd better tell me everything!" he said.

Soon, Peter knew the whole story. A graphic description by Sandy and Adam, with a realistic re-enactment by Tessa of creeping through the grass to reach Derek Bute and Cecil, left all of them laughing, including Peter.

"What a cheek that man's got!" Peter said, heatedly, when at last they had got over their laughter at Tessa's antics. "And," he added, trying to look at them sternly, but failing, "I'm beginning to wonder what sort of helpers I have here! Bribery —"

"But Peter!" Exasperated, Sandy blurted out,

"I've been trying to tell the others – and you. It wasn't really bribery because Tess and I have discovered that Derek Bute didn't really pay anything for Cecil – and he doesn't want him. He's *glad* we've found a home for him!"

Sandy looked round at the others, triumphantly, but Chrissy looked doubtful.

"But you haven't really *got* a home for him, have you?" she said. "And why did Derek Bute try to steal Cecil if he doesn't want him?" she added.

"He just wanted to steal back the evidence," Sandy explained. "He knew he'd been acting against the law when he tethered Cecil like he did. And I *have* got a home for Cecil," she added, pulling Aunt Cress's letter from her jodhpurs pocket. "This is from my aunt," she explained. "She's got a donkey sanctuary at Santon. It's about fifty miles away, on the coast. She says Cecil can go there and stay for the rest of his life. She's sending a horsebox for him next week." Sandy looked at Tessa, Adam, Sarah and Andrea. "Aunt Cress says there's room for six in the box – that's Cecil and five ponies. We can take the ponies and stay with her, and then ride home. We can have our long ride, after all!" Sandy finished delightedly.

Everything seemed to happen on Wednesday.

Sandy and Tessa were the first of the helpers to arrive at Heronsway. When they had stowed their two bicycles away in the haybarn, they made their way to the stables. Duskie's stable was the first on their route. The black pony was watching with pricked ears. He whinnied delightedly

109

as Tessa approached, and she soon disappeared into the stable. Quest had seen Sandy arrive at the haybarn, and was pawing the ground impatiently already. She whickered softly, tossing her long fine mane as she moved her head from side to side.

Excitement spun in Sandy's mind as she remembered, again, that today was the day of the expedition to Santon. In the saddlebag of her bicycle was a haversack packed with a few items of clothing. Rainwear was packed in, just in case — although the weather forecast was good for at least the next week. Also in her pocket was a hoofpick and a small first-aid box.

As Sandy groomed the chestnut pony, brushing down Quest's already shining hindquarters, she could hear whistling and singing coming from the direction of the yard. Pausing, she looked out through the opening above the stable door. At the end of the other row of stables, Tessa's head appeared, too.

"It's Chrissy!" Tessa called, pointing a body-brush in the direction of the feed room.

"She sounds cheerful!" Sandy commented, and then Chrissy appeared in the feed-room doorway. She waved a piece of paper at them, grinning widely and dancing on the spot.

Tessa leaned her elbows on the top of Duskie's door.

"Obviously it's all been too much for her!" she called across the yard, winking exaggeratedly at Sandy.

"It's come!" Chrissy shrieked, dancing round again. "It's come! I've done it! I'm an Assistant Instructor!"

Tessa and Sandy hardly had time to congratulate Chrissy before everyone else came. Soon there was an excited gathering in the yard; Adam joined them, closely followed by Andrea and Sarah.

They hardly noticed Sue arrive, holding onto Peter's arm.

"So this is what it's like while I'm away," Sue said, laughing. "Lots of noise and no work!"

Sue had been right. There wasn't much work done that morning, apart from the essential feeding, mucking-out and exercising routine. No lessons had been arranged for the morning, in honour of Sue's homecoming, so Chrissy was able to join in the festivities in the coffee bar.

Sue, delighted at being back at Heronsway again, insisted on making the coffee, and produced two large boxes of cream cakes.

"This isn't going to be an everyday occurrence," she assured them, smiling, "but *I'm* going to be here every day, from now on – that's for sure!"

While Peter handed round the cakes, Sue delved into a carrier bag and pulled out seven packets.

"I bought you one each," Sue said, holding up a tee-shirt from one of the packets. "There's one for Kate, too. They're to thank you for all your help," she added. The shirts had galloping horses careering across the front and "Heronsway Helper" written across the back.

"I ordered them before I was ill," Sue admitted, "and they're only just finished. I'm going to sell some in the coffee bar," she told them, "but those

111

will say Heronsway Equestrian Centre. These are special presents for our helpers."

A horsebox pulled up outside, tooting, and interrupting Sue.

Sandy jumped up. "I forgot all about Cecil!" she cried.

"Don't worry," said Sue, "he's still there – I saw him on our way down the drive."

The next hour was a busy one. Puffin and Rags were loaded into the box, followed by Duskie and Cindy. Then Cecil had to be persuaded that the horsebox was a safe place for a little grey donkey – and he wasn't too sure about it. Quest soon dispelled his doubts by bounding up the ramp to lead him in.

Sandy put an arm round Quest's neck, rubbing her just under the mane, which she always liked. The beautiful chestnut mare turned her head, pushing her soft nose against Sandy's arm.

"We're off to Aunt Cress's," Sandy whispered into the pony's ear. "Our first adventure together."

Quest's large liquid eyes looked at Sandy wisely, and the pony snorted impatiently, shaking her head so that her long fine mane fell untidily on her shining chestnut neck.